Friends in High Places

It's pouring with rain in New York City, and just over the Brooklyn Bridge three men wait in Rita Noonan's apartment . . . Standing together near her bed are homicide detective Lenny Morris — asthmatic, several pounds overweight and counting — and Jesus Rantz, his leering, chain-smoking partner. The third is William "Wilsey" Weiss, friend of her ex-husband and former police officer, lying face down dead with bullet holes in his head. Thus begins Rita's second case, perhaps a little too close to home for a woman who's just been made partner in Malcolm Ortner's private investigation agency.

Over a decade earlier, Wilsey began his descent into a life of drugs and deceit. Until the night before his murder, neither Rita nor Frank, her former husband, had heard from the sandy-haired ex-cop. Evidently, sometime between then and the previous evening, when he'd arrived in a cold sweat at Rita's apartment, Wilsey had found out too much about too many people, especially certain police officers.

In her struggle to restore the agency's reputation amid the hindrances of partner Malcolm Ortner's ailing health and roving eye, Rita finds herself drawn into the seedy, drug-infested neighborhoods of Manhattan's Lower East Side; into an inner circle of the police force that seems to be run on its own agenda; to Queens, where ex-husband Frank hopes for a reunion of sorts; and, ultimately, into the crossfire between a case and her career . . .

In the tradition of Sue Grafton's Kinsey Millhone mysteries, *Friends in High Places* brings to life an intelligent female sleuth who tackles a tough caseload and all the pressures facing a single woman working in Manhattan. Rita's sharp insight and wry sensibility make *Friends in High Places* a strong follow-up to *Money to Burn* and firmly establish Michael Hendricks as a novelist to watch.

Friends in High Places

Michael Hendricks

MACMILLAN
LONDON

First published in the United States of America 1991 by
Charles Scribner's Sons, New York

First published in the United Kingdom 1991 by
MACMILLAN LONDON LIMITED
a division of Macmillan Publishers Limited
Cavaye Place London SW10 9PG
and Basingstoke

Associated companies in Auckland, Delhi, Dublin, Gaborone,
Hamburg, Harare, Hong Kong, Johannesburg, Kuala Lumpur, Lagos,
Manzini, Melbourne, Mexico City, Nairobi, New York, Singapore
and Tokyo

ISBN 0-333-54867-1

A CIP catalogue record for this book is available from the British Library

Printed and bound in Great Britain by Billing and Sons Limited, Worcester

For Dorothy and Klaus

ONE

♦

Wilsey was dead. He was facedown, taking up most of the floor space of my tiny apartment. The few pieces of cookware I'd accumulated over the years had been thrown from the kitchen, forming an obstacle course in the small front hallway. The contents of my bookshelves lay scattered on the floor, soaking up whatever there was left of Wilsey to soak up. The cops were so crammed in around the king-size bed that filled my studio, I could only imagine what was going on in the bathroom.

I took another step inside and got a closer look. He'd been shot in the head. Execution-style, they called it. Only it looked like the executioner didn't quite have the nerve to pull the trigger when Wilsey was kneeling there waiting to get it. The gun must have swayed a little to the side. The first shot only cracked open his head. Knocked him on his face. Probably knocked him senseless, too. Whoever it was needed a second shot to finish the job, straight through the back of the head and into the floor.

"I hope the guy was alone."

Lenny Morris was half of a Manhattan homicide team that had worked together since back when Frank and I were still married. Out here in Brooklyn, they were a long way from home. Lenny was the bigger half, pushing at whatever weight limits the force still had in these days of equal opportunity. He'd put on some extra poundage every year I'd known him and lately he'd picked up some asthma to go with it. Thinning red hair. Red skin. Always sweating. The guy shook even when standing still. Right now, he was shaking over Wilsey.

Jesus Rantz, the other half of the team, finished the thought as if it had been his to begin with.

"He'd sure as hell catch shit if he wasn't. Can you imagine? Son of a bitch can't even ice somebody when they're kneeling there waiting for it. Shit."

Then a laugh. No humor, but a laugh anyway. They weren't talking to anyone. It was shoptalk. Something to say.

That was when they must have noticed me. They turned, almost together, as in some choreographed dance. I always kind of liked Morris. Rantz was just a jerk. Right now I wasn't too happy about seeing either of them.

"What's going on here, Rita?"

"I don't know."

"You don't know? What don't you know? What was Wilsey doing here? Why was he killed? When did you last see him? How did he get here? Where have you been for the last few hours? What don't you know, Rita?"

"Shut up, Jesus. Leave her alone." Lenny wheezed between each word. "Come on. Let's go grab a cup of coffee someplace. I think I saw a coffee shop down the block."

It was a good idea. Between the photographer, the print dusters, the cop retrieving bullets, the cop charting the room, the medical examiner, and a couple of other guys just standing around looking official, there wasn't much room for an interrogation. Besides, even though they were all giving me the professional courtesy of assuming I wasn't squeamish around a body, even the body of someone I knew, the truth was, they saw a lot more of this kind of thing than I did, and right now I just wanted to get out.

When I'd called the office and Malcolm told me to go

straight home, I'd only heard there was some trouble. That seemed peculiar, considering I lived alone. Still, I hadn't expected this. And despite Morris's superficial friendliness, neither he nor Rantz wanted to give me time to pull myself together.

"I don't understand, Rita. You say you don't see the guy for nine years. Next thing you know, he shows up dead in your apartment, and somebody's torn the place apart in the bargain. It doesn't sit with me. You're a detective. Does it sit with you? Cream or sugar?"

Lenny pushed the aluminum creamer across the Formica with his stubby little fingers. I'd lived across the street from this place for years, but this was the first time I'd been inside. I couldn't foresee any urgent reason to come back.

"I didn't say I hadn't seen him in nine years. I saw him yesterday. He stopped by yesterday."

He'd shown up, out of the blue. For three years he'd been a fixture at our place. Frank's protégé on the job. The hot young cop. Then he'd been kicked off the force. A couple of years later Frank and I split up. I never saw Wilsey again. Till last night. And now again this afternoon.

"Hey, sure. Nine years. Yesterday. What's the difference?"

Rantz snorted with disgust, then opened one of those fancy boxes of European cigarettes, the brown ones, and lit up. He probably said he smoked them for the flavor. Probably read *Hustler* for the articles, too. Lenny ignored him as though he was used to ignoring him.

"He stopped by yesterday? Just like that. Did he want something?"

I was only half-hearing the questions, as if Lenny were talking on a bad connection from halfway around the world. All I could think of was the way Wilsey'd looked. Not just now. In a way, that was easier to deal with. But last night he'd seemed changed. Not even a trace of the up-and-coming kid. He was dirty. Unkempt. Bad teeth. No different from any other junkie in the city. Except he was supposed to be someone I knew.

Lenny sipped from his coffee. We were two friends having a conversation over a coffee break. What a saint. It was good cop, bad cop. I knew it. They knew I knew it. I wasn't bothered. They'd been doing it so long they probably couldn't help themselves. Besides, it was working.

"He rang up from the street. I let him in. He was traveling, on the road, a courier service or something. He ran out of money and needed a place to stay."

This time I took the sip of coffee. It was a good time for a pause. Time to remember this wasn't just chitchat and I wasn't some witness. No one had explicitly called me a suspect yet, but they hadn't told me they'd caught whoever did it either. Right now the questions were the only way to find out where I stood.

"So he was staying at your place. That's how he got in there?"

I could see Rantz's eyebrows move just enough to know he was thinking about there being only one bed and no place else for anyone to sleep in my apartment.

"I told him to leave."

"You didn't see the guy for nine years, he comes to you needing help, and you told him to fuck off?" Rantz was talking almost to himself, leaving it up to me to decide if he didn't believe me or just thought I was one hell of a dependable friend. He shook his head and exhaled cigarette smoke for effect.

"I gave him some money for a hotel."

"Aren't you wonderful?"

"Look, Lenny, I don't have to listen to this guy. If you're

going to make this harder than it has to be, I'll get a lawyer and you'll see just how hard it can be."

I was firm, not shrill. Trying to take the threat out of my voice. Lenny was a nice guy, but he was still a cop and cops don't like taking orders.

"Lighten up, Jesus."

Rantz rolled his eyes, took another hit off the cigarette, and looked across the room to check out the butt of our waitress, a sixteen-year-old Puerto Rican girl in bicycle shorts. The girl gave him a dirty look. He didn't notice. Lenny shook his head sadly, like he was really distressed about the whole thing.

"Look, Rita. We're all a little tense. Wilsey was a cop. An ex-cop, sure. But he was a cop from our precinct. You know the kind of pressure we'll be under. It's no good. You want another cup?"

I shook my head. That explained what Rantz and Morris were doing here. It also meant they had no suspects. At least, no one other than me.

"I think I'll get one."

He signaled the waitress, ordered another coffee, and asked her to throw on a hamburger while she was at it. Rantz did nothing to move his eyes as the poor girl came toward us.

"Are you sure you don't want something?"

I was sure.

The interrogation continued. They wanted to know where I'd been. I thought about telling them the truth, about how I'd been staking out a postal worker for his wife, and just before I'd called in to the office, I'd snapped off a roll of film of the guy putting it to one of the domestic help in the Tropical Room at the adult motel on his route, only I didn't want to get Rantz all worked up. I told them I'd been working a surveillance case and could prove it, but that I'd just as soon not involve the person who was my alibi until it was absolutely necessary because it would compromise my case. They bought it. Conditionally.

They asked if I knew what Wilsey's business in New York was, if I knew why he decided to look me up, if I knew what he was involved in, if I knew why anyone would bring him back to my apartment to kill him, if I knew what they were looking for in my apartment—all the questions I would have asked if I were in their place. I shook my head each time and told them I didn't know.

We stayed at the coffee shop over an hour and a half. Enough time for Lenny to down five cups of coffee, two hamburgers, and three orders of fries. They asked all the same questions again in fifteen different ways, hoping to catch me in a lie, a contradiction, or at least to jog my memory to come up with something I'd initially forgotten. But I stuck to my answers, and I didn't remember anything, and we all knew that sooner or later they'd have to charge me or let me go.

Only then did it begin to sink in what had happened. Wilsey would be gone by now, but I wouldn't need to see him again to remember his caved-in skull, his open, lifeless eyes. It's a lie that dead eyes stare. Wilsey's eyes hadn't stared. With a vengeance, they hadn't stared. His hand had reached pointlessly into the air. His mouth was open. And of course there was the blood. The blood would still be there. On my carpet, on my blanket, on anything that landed on the floor next to Wilsey. The police take the blood they need, but they don't provide a cleaning service to get rid of the rest of it.

I got up to leave. Lenny wiped some of the catsup from his lip with a napkin.

"Hey, Rita," Rantz said. "You remember that courier service? You have a name?"

"No. Why?"

"Wilsey wasn't just passing through. He lived in New York. The Lower East Side. He never left." If he wanted a reaction, I didn't give him one. "Now let's just say you've been telling the truth. If I were you, I'd start thinking about why he got in touch with you just now and why someone wants to tie you into his death." He paused. "And if you're lying, I'm going to nail you to the wall." He licked his lips suggestively as though he wanted me to be lying.

"Don't worry about the check," Lenny popped in. "I'll pick it up. Do you want me to say hi to Frank?"

There was no need to answer. I could feel Rantz's eyes following me all the way to the door and did my best to take all the swing out of my hips. It didn't work. It wasn't about the swing. It never was.

"Looking good, Rita. Hey, did you ever think whoever it was might have been looking for you. I mean, I hope you're not worried about someone coming back for more."

I should have responded. Put the jerk in his place. Only nothing clever came to mind. I was already putting one foot in front of the other. Heading home. To take it back from break-ins, from murder, from the police. I had to clean every trace of Wilsey from my apartment. And I had to try to remember a kid with funny hair, a chipped-tooth smile, and those pale blue eyes.

TWO

◆

It was a long time ago. Only a couple of years after my big move to the city. Before I'd ever heard about Malcolm and the agency, before I'd even thought about getting my investigator's license, when I was still doing office temp work and wondering if I'd made the right decision, moving in with the cop who'd come to investigate a break-in at my apartment. It was back when I must have still had enough hope for Frank to marry him. And back when Frank still made friends on the job.

William "Wilsey" Weiss was new to the department. He stood about five feet eight, with one of those compact, well-balanced bodies you see on wrestlers, real wrestlers. He was probably the same age as all the other rookies, but Wilsey always seemed like a kid. His thick, sand-colored hair could have been cut down to a crew and somewhere in there a piece of it would still be sticking out. Some time back he'd chipped a tooth, giving him a lopsided, mischievous grin. Only Wilsey's eyes, a pale, weak, washed-out blue, kept him from being the *Boy's Life* poster boy.

From the beginning, Frank and Stub Kinnon, his partner, would come home with stories about this funny kid at work. It wasn't that Wilsey's rookie year was so remarkable. He made the usual mistakes, the usual successes. The remarkable part was everyone's perception of that performance. Two rookies would bust dealers on the same day in the same precinct. No big deal. No instantly recognizable names. No gunplay. No drama. But somehow with Wilsey there'd always be a twist. Losing a shoe on a chase. Stumbling onto a ring of grandmother dealers. Something. So where one rookie would get a clap on the back and spend the rest of the day writing up arrest reports, lieutenants would write Wilsey up for commendations and find themselves retelling the kid's adventures several times over beers that night with Wilsey's sergeant. More than that, Wilsey's charm wasn't limited to higher-ups. Odds were, the other rookie himself would be overheard in the locker room: "Say, did you hear about Wilsey's bust today?"—shaking his head all the while in astonishment.

The fun kept up for the whole year, only people like Wilsey don't disappear in a system. There's no twenty years on the force accompanied by a couple of promotions with an early retirement at full pay. Sooner or later, somebody notices them, assumes they're wasting their time doing whatever everyone else is doing, and thinks up something special to take advantage of their talents. For Wilsey that something was undercover investigations. They wined him, dined him, and got him to trade the uniform in for civilian clothes, then sat back and waited for the even better stories this screwy kid would bring back now.

Wilsey didn't disappoint. His first case was busting up a protection racket in the Garment District. The brass gave him a crash course in how the industry works, provided him with a résumé, and landed him a job in shipping with a sportswear company specializing in women's swimsuits.

Some hoods had been muscling into businesses along Fashion Avenue, hustling payouts in exchange for not torching inventories, not delaying deliveries. There were the usual threats of broken bones and revealing design secrets to the trade. Since there'd been a couple of suspicious fires in the area, Wilsey's job was to identify who the hoods were and who, if anyone, was backing them up.

It took Wilsey six and a half weeks to find out that the two hoods were operating on their own, taking advantage of someone else's fires to inspire the fear they needed to conduct their business. He also nailed the two bankrupt designers and their hired firebug who'd torched the buildings in the first place, busted three sweatshops, and redesigned his employer's delivery system to increase efficiency and cut thousands from the budget. The case wound up just before his big promotion was due.

Once again he was the talk of the locker room.

"Did you hear about that promotion?"

"Fuckin' Wilsey."

Frank and Stub were Wilsey's contacts on the operation and they'd all get together socially. Frank would invite them over at least once a week—Stub, the good old Southern boy whose marriage was on the rocks and who was always up for a good time, and Wilsey, the sweet kid who'd always bring a present. A bottle of wine. Some flowers. Maybe a paperback. They'd eat their dinner, then head to the nearest pub to blow off the rest of the night. At least, that was always the story.

The night the rag-trade thing wound up, they'd gone out drinking along with a few guys Frank figured couldn't hurt Wilsey's career. It was a real place, not just a cop hangout. Wilsey had his smile working. He had the tousled hair. He had the full line of stories. And he had Frank, the seasoned professional, and Stub, the much-decorated daredevil, backing him up. The kid had department superstar status waiting for him on a platter. It wasn't until the others left that Frank realized Wilsey'd also had twice as much to drink as everyone else, that Wilsey had something to say about the people who designed situations for others to go undercover in, that he felt like a freak the way people wanted to meet him, that he hated the people he worked for, the people he worked with, and the people whose trust he had to betray in order to do his job.

Frank never held it against the kid. Everyone hates his job. What's wrong with that? Frank probably never would have trusted him if he'd claimed to love it. And drinking buddies just weren't that easy to find. Even so, Frank and Stub left when Wilsey picked a fight with four commodities traders who looked like they'd received their training on the playing fields of Mississippi State. When Wilsey showed up the next day with a puffy cheek and a couple of busted ribs, Frank just laughed it off and vowed to watch who he brought along whenever he went drinking with Wilsey.

Next on Wilsey's list was a chop shop in the Bronx. Two months under cover, tearing down motors, stripping cars for parts. Wilsey turned out to be a mechanical natural. He had such a way with transmissions, he even built up the garage's legitimate business. That's when Wilsey made his first mob contacts.

Wilsey would say he had no family in the area and they'd invite him home for dinner. Real pals. They liked him, just like the cops liked him. One weekend, after he'd worked around the clock to clear the garage before a feared raid, one big shot even bought him a Coupe de Ville and set him up for a night in Atlantic City complete with young ladies.

Wilsey's job in the chop shop was such a hit, Frank got the force to bring in a second undercover so they wouldn't have to expose Wilsey when it came time for the bust. And Wilsey didn't let Frank down. From the chop shop he went on to open up a gambling ring. Then a stolen-property operation, a call-girl/escort service, and, finally, drugs. Never once did he end up testifying in a bust; the force would wait till he'd moved on before they'd take the operation down.

Frank just kept feeding Wilsey whatever he'd need to rise higher in the organization. Meeting every few days, usually in a bar, Frank stopped trying to bring along the top-level boys. And when Stub busted his leg falling through the roof of an abandoned building where some kids had stuck an old dog to starve, Frank began to meet Wilsey alone. He'd tell Wilsey it was for security reasons. There was no need for more people to know Wilsey than was absolutely necessary. Even if you could trust them, it just increased the odds that eventually someone would see Wilsey with a cop. It was Frank's job to make sure Wilsey's accomplishments were noticed, and since the commendations continued to come, Wilsey trusted that Frank was doing that job.

But security was only one of the reasons Frank wanted to shield Wilsey from the rest of the department. Almost any-time they got together, Wilsey had a drink in his hand, and when they met in a bar, Wilsey would have already had a few before Frank even got there. Frank would talk all the time about how he was going to say something to Wilsey for his own good, how the drinking could only hurt his career, how it might even get him in trouble, but Frank wasn't that kind of guy. The conversation never took place. Wilsey would have to take care of himself.

There must have been more to Frank's uneasiness than the drinking, though. Frank had been around the depart-ment long enough to know that plenty of careers had flour-ished despite a fondness for the bottle. What drove Frank crazy was what happened when Wilsey drank. There were more confessions. Stories from childhood that most people would forget or at least let lie. The kinds of things that embarrassed Frank even to think about. There were more fights in which Wilsey was always overmatched or outnumbered. And now there were boasts. The names of the guys he was buddying up with. The gifts he'd received. The women he slept with. And something unspoken. Partying. A word he'd use with the expectation that no further explanation would be requested.

Then Wilsey started seeing one of the girls he'd been managing. It wasn't one of those cop-whore relationships you read about. The noble officer brought low by a profane love for an evil, seductive woman. Love never entered the picture with Wilsey and Lena. It wasn't even passion or the party-girl good times Stub fell for. Addiction was more like it. Wilsey losing contact with Frank for weeks at a time, finally showing up pale, worn-out, with some vague story of a trip or a meeting or a plan and always with the promise of delivering something big next time.

Lena didn't last. There was the one meeting when Wilsey showed up talking about how he'd brought her home to meet his three-generation cop family. Frank couldn't tell if Wilsey was more pleased about humiliating Lena or his mother. Wilsey was losing control. There was no more impish grin. No more cocky attitude. He'd burnt out and Frank had to get him out. Only, when Frank suggested withdrawing him from the operation, Wilsey exploded. There was a fight. He claimed to be close to something. He begged to stay in place.

For the next several weeks Wilsey managed to pull himself together. He dressed better. He took better care of himself. Maybe he even slept a little. The lights came back to his eyes. He showed up for his check-in meetings on time with all the information necessary to convince Frank to keep him on the job.

Then came Toni. And, after her, Dina. Wilsey was out of control. Frank asked for a reassignment, a change. He had to pull strings, calling in a favor from one of the higher-ups who owed him. Switching away from undercover narcotics. All for a change.

It wouldn't look strange on his record. Cops transferred all the time. They traded favors all the time. Only, Frank had never called in favors. He had this theory that favors existed out there like threads. And if he helped out enough people over the years, pulling extra duty, covering for a partner with his wife, sooner or later those threads would form a blanket, and that blanket would keep him warm if he ever got cold. The key was leaving those threads out there. And now he'd called one of those threads back.

Frank only heard about Wilsey off and on after that. He was working some heavy drug case, taking down a protection racket, infiltrating the gangs. Big guns were going to fall. They'd nail this year's Mr. Big. Wilsey'd pull it off, surface in triumph, and return a golden boy once again.

"Did you hear how Wilsey took down the whole mob by himself?" someone would ask.

"Fuckin' Wilsey."

Only the bust never came. There was a problem. Frank never talked about it. Wilsey the cop surfaced. Or rather, he was extricated. He was nailed with something the force referred to publicly as entrapment; privately, as crossing over the line. Whether it was selling dope, pocketing money, getting hooked himself, or something else, if Frank knew, he never spoke about it.

One night there was a knock on the door. Wilsey was there. Strung out. Crying. He was facing charges. He might do time. It was raining that night, just like it was now. He stood there in the kitchen, dripping, and crying. I sat on the corner of my bed, trying to disappear, trying not to listen, and saw for myself all the changes Frank had been talking about. The dark circles under his eyes, the weight loss, the nerves. Frank tried to throw him out, but there was that kid, the kid who'd screwed up, and before he'd leave, he made Frank promise to do what he could to help.

And Frank followed through, calling in still more favors, more threads. Unraveling the blanket he'd been weaving since he'd been on the job. This time the blanket unraveled big-time. Wilsey never went down. There were no charges. There were only two conditions. For the department, Wilsey had to resign. He left the force with no hope of receiving a recommendation to work as a cop again. The other condition was Frank's. He'd cut the tie. There was to be no communication between them again. He never wanted to hear from Wilsey, never wanted to see him. He'd done what he'd done. Now he wanted to forget about it.

And that was that. Frank never saw Wilsey again. He never again spoke about his blanket of security. He never even complained about how his career suddenly dead-ended after the Wilsey incident. He'd done what he'd done. He'd forgotten about it, he said. But after Stub got himself killed coming through a door too soon on a buy-and-bust operation a couple of years later, Frank cut the friendship stuff out altogether.

I hadn't thought of Wilsey in years. Not until he showed up at my door, dropping in just like he had years ago. Only now the transformation was complete. There were no illusions about what he was becoming. He'd already become it.

He'd done his best to act as if this were old times. Just like I had. As though if we acted like nothing had changed, we could avoid the awkwardness of the present moment. He'd even brought a present. A couple of books wrapped in brown paper that I'd decided not to mention to Rantz and Morris until I was sure the books were still in the apartment.

The rest happened just like I'd told them. Except for near the end when he'd started crying. Blaming Frank for abandoning him. Letting him go just when he'd needed Frank most. And then he'd left.

The police cars were gone from in front of my building. Wilsey would be gone, too. Theoretically, I could go in now. Theoretically, things could start getting back to normal.

THREE

◆

No matter how many ploys he'd used to get himself invited over since I'd started working for him, Malcolm had never before been to my apartment. Tonight his dreams would come true. I'd called to explain what was going on. I owed him that much. He'd taken the call from the police in the first place and he'd have to find out eventually. Besides, needed a shoulder to cry on and his was the best available. hadn't expected him to leave the office. I hadn't particularly expected him even to pop his chair out of the recline mode. Murders, however, were special for Malcolm. They made him feel like a real detective again.

"Stay where you are. I'll be right over."

No thought about the torrential downpour. No thought about the late hour he'd be returning to Manhattan. No thought about the three flights of stairs he'd be climbing.

"I'll be right over."

By the time he arrived, soaked and out of breath, I'd already cleaned most of the apartment. Everything that had been thrown on the floor was back on the shelves. Everything covered with blood was washed, twice, or stripped and piled in a corner. No way was I going to sleep on sheet splattered by Wilsey, whether I could still see the blood or not. It didn't matter how little money I had in the bank, new sheets I could afford.

The only place I couldn't clean was the bed. There was blood on the box springs that wouldn't come up with water, soap, or anything. I tried to recall some helpful hint for blood removal, but all my Aunt Sallies must have kept that sort of thing to themselves, or maybe there just weren't that many Aunt Sallies around anymore. I would either have to get rid of the only piece of furniture I owned or learn to sleep with Wilsey.

The door was locked. A bolt and a chain. Even so, I could hear Malcolm's heavy wheezing and gasping for air from the landing below. He hadn't buzzed up from the street-level intercom, so he must have come in the building when someone was leaving. Just the kind of safety feature I demanded for a living space. The kind I was relying on to keep the creeps out should they decide to come back. I opened the door and saw Malcolm propped against a wall, one flight to go, broken out in a sweat.

"You okay?"

"I'm just taking care of myself," he said between heaves, then stalled some more. "Best thing ever happened to me was that heart attack. Eat right, stay fit, take care of myself. You could learn something yourself."

Next he'd be advising me to have one myself. The old guy'd been talking up his remarkable recovery and good health ever since he'd come back from the hospital. I never asked how chocolate Danish fit into his eat-right shtick.

"Do you want me to help?"

"I'm taking care of myself."

He still hadn't made a move away from the wall, although his breathing was coming a little easier.

"Well, then, just wait there until you catch your breath."

"I'm fine."

For the seven years I'd worked for him Malcolm had dreamed of getting invited over to my apartment. Whatever else the fantasy might have included, I'm sure it also included an elevator. Malcolm started up the stairs one more time. One step at a time. Holding on to the railing the whole way. Lifting one foot. Bringing the other to meet it. Then resting before he had to lift that foot and start the whole process over again.

It took ten minutes for him to make it up that last flight. I went inside so he didn't have to suffer my watching his ordeal. I'd never known Malcolm before his heart condition, so I didn't have much to compare him to. He might have been something in his prime. But this was awful. And lately he'd gotten worse. He'd need a pill when he got here. I filled a glass of water, left it on the counter, and went to sit on the bed.

"So what happened here, Rita?"

He was in the apartment, sitting on the folding chair and as focused as he could be with his face three shades of purple and sweat rolling down his neck onto his collar. While Malcolm caught his breath as best he could, I went on with my story, the same story I'd given Morris and Rantz, only this time I didn't leave out the part about the books.

"I don't like you being associated with a shmuck like that. Why did he come here?"

"I don't know."

"Tell me again what he said when he showed up."

Malcolm was on the case now, looking at the floor as I told him word for word everything I remembered about Wilsey's visit. Everything about the courier job. Everything about his traveling. About his being broke. About his needing a place to stay. About Frank's abandoning him. About how the cops thought it was all lies. Malcolm never looked up, making sure he wouldn't be distracted by the fact that he was finally alone in my apartment with me and this huge bed that taunted him the entire time I spoke because he was bothering with something as trivial as a murder.

He sat there for a while in silence after I spoke, then shook his head and sighed.

"You have another glass of water, maybe?"

I poured him the glass, even cracking open some fresh ice cubes from a freezer badly in need of defrosting.

"You want to see the books?"

"There's something in them?"

"Malcolm, if there is, I swear I couldn't find it."

He shrugged and took the books. I was almost disappointed when I'd found them. It knocked the only thing I could figure that tied me or my apartment to Wilsey right out of the picture. Who knew? Maybe the pages were made of pressed cocaine. Maybe there was some microfilm of weapon plans that would threaten the safety of the free world. But they were right with all the other books. Trashed on the floor. I was about as sure as I could be that they'd passed through the hands of the killer. But they were still here.

Malcolm first looked the books over, taking in cover, title, author, whatever else could be of value. He turned the books upside down and shook them to see if anything fell out. After that he began the tedious process of paging through each book leaf by leaf. Were there any marks on the pages? Had anything been stuck to a page? He never looked up. Didn't speak, except once.

"Were there any books on top of these?"

"They were kind of in the middle of a pile."

"Then whoever came here didn't find what he was looking for either."

If I'd said something like that, it would have meant I was about to give up. Malcolm kept going. Page by page. Looking for whatever it was the killer missed. Already knowing it wasn't there. He just kept looking. It was a side of investigating I still had trouble with. The one-foot-in-front-of-the-other, cover-every-base perseverance Malcolm had trained into his body. There was nothing to do but stand back, watch, and admire.

"It's not there, is it?"

Malcolm shook his head, still eyeing the books suspiciously.

"What?"

"Whatever the guy who killed Wilsey wanted."

"I don't know. Maybe we should check the spine."

He was holding the book on end, checking for any signs of tampering. Even Malcolm looked about ready to forgo the search.

"This is what he gave you? These two books? Just like this?"

"They were wrapped in brown paper."

"Where's the paper?"

He was grasping at straws. That didn't make me feel any better about what I had to tell him.

"I threw it out."

"You threw it out?"

"I didn't know he was going to be murdered when he gave it to me."

"Jesus."

He threw the books on the floor.

I suddenly felt very tired. What I imagined it felt like when you got doped and the drugs first started to hit. The image was a little romantic. People didn't dope much anymore. If they wanted you out of the way, even temporarily, they killed you. But, hey, that's what an imagination's all about.

We went over the story again and again, until Malcolm stood up, went to the sink, and poured himself another glass of water. This time when he came back, he parked his bulky frame on the bed he'd been eyeing since he got there.

"What are you thinking?"

I wasn't sure what he was asking. He was probably hoping murders got me going and he'd finally get lucky. As if to confirm my suspicions, he dropped back on his elbows in a semireclined position.

"I think I should work the case."

Malcolm rubbed his face. He knew what I was thinking. I was a partner now. People knew it. Maybe not people walking down the street, but in the business: "Hey, Ortner took himself a partner. A broad. Ortner."

We'd never spoken about what being a woman meant to the company. Normally, it didn't mean much. But what it meant right now was that I had to be good. At least I couldn't screw up. Not big-time. This was big-time. Who was going to bring their problems to an investigator who had people murdered in her apartment without doing anything about it? And it wasn't only the good jobs that would disappear. We'd be lucky to bring in the divorce work either. It was tacky. It didn't reflect well on the agency. My agency.

But if Malcolm was reading me, I was reading him, too. I'd called it a case, but this Wilsey thing only qualified as such because it was a crime. A case was different. A case was an assignment. Something someone paid us to work on. Something that kept the agency solvent. Sure, a reputation was important. But as far as Malcolm was concerned, his was the only one that mattered. The partnership was a concession he'd made only because of his health. The agency was still his baby. The last thing we needed was to put me out of commission chasing down leads on a situation that could only end up costing us money.

"I don't know, Rita. Do the police have any leads?"

"Not that they told me."

"Still, maybe we should give them some time. We'll keep you on a low profile. There's a woman with some divorce work coming in tomorrow. You're good at that. You call and tell them about the books here. Say you forgot or something. We'll see what happens."

And that was that. Malcolm had done what he came to do. And there was no reason to stay. Other than that it had actually gotten late. It was still raining. Hard. And there was still this huge bed in my apartment. I looked at the old man in the chair and prepared for the thousandth time to deflect the advance, hopefully before it even came to a direct confrontation.

Only the advance never came. He looked down wistfully at the bed he was sitting on and gave it something of a love pat. But that was as far as it got. He popped one more of his pills down with the last slug of his water, then gave me a hug and a kiss like he would give his sister if he'd had one, and left. No fight. No struggle. Not even any interest. I didn't miss it. I just wasn't prepared for the vacuum.

I waited for a good half hour for Malcolm to get himself down the stairs and off the block, then bundled up the pile of bloody sheets, walked them outside to a trash can, and tossed them. It was the only way I could even hope to sleep tonight.

FOUR

♦

I woke in the morning and the bloodstain on the box spring was still there. I ate a bowl of the same cereal I'd been forcing down my throat since I'd read articles telling how it would save my life. I read the same newspaper I always read, expecting the whole time to find an article in it telling me that the cereal would kill me. But it was a new day. Wilsey was dead. I'd cleaned my apartment. And life went on.

Malcolm had told me to let the cops handle things and, on that advice, I set out to drop off the two books at the precinct: "I'm sorry, Officer. I don't know how I could have forgotten about them. I was just so upset, I guess."

I was hoping I'd be able to sell the story to Morris rather than Rantz, but there was no such luck. He was even alone in the drab detective office. A hard little man who wanted so badly to project a street attitude, he had probably really been raised in some upscale suburb and was only working out a little mommy-daddy resentment on the rest of us.

I handed him the books and waited for the hassling that was bound to follow. Only it never came. Rantz just gave me a dirty look, took a hit from his brown cigarette, and took the books.

"Weiss gave these to you?"

I nodded and that was that. No threats about concealing evidence. Nothing. Just another hit off that cigarette, a mumbled thanks, and a brush-off.

The movie was over. I could forget it ever happened and go back to work. There was even a case waiting for me. Hannah Lowell walked into the office before I had a chance to take off my coat. Just a shade under five feet tall, with lustrous black hair, wet red lips, a pair of heels begging to be pushed over, and a blue silk dress packed to overflowing with whatever it was that could possibly overflow from a dress, she walked like she expected every woman in the world to hate her and every man to kiss her ass. With only Malcolm and me in the office, we easily met both expectations.

Hannah looked directly at Malcolm, smiled seductively, and asked, "Is Malcolm Ortner here?"

For sixty-seven years Malcolm had been dreaming about a woman like this knocking on his door and asking for him. Maybe it was a little late in the game. Maybe in the dream he still had hair, weighed a lot less and didn't have to take his heart into consideration when he got excited. Still, a dream is a dream. He dropped the Danish he was eating, pushed his hulking frame so that his reclining chair rocked forward, brushed the crumbs off his chest, and rose to greet his guest.

"I'm Malcolm Ortner. How can I help you?"

Immediately, one arm was around her shoulder as he guided her to the only free chair in the room, the new one, the one with the rollers, the one without any stains or any stuffing popping out of it, the one I'd bought, walking past me like I wasn't there. It wouldn't occur to Malcolm to introduce me as his partner. I made a mental note for a procedures discussion to be taken up later.

"This is very personal."

Her voice was breathy, with a slight trace of Jersey or Brooklyn in it. Take your pick.

"Rita, could you run out and get us a cup of coffee."

It was the point in the movie where the line "Smile when

you say that, pardner" belonged. Not only wasn't Malcolm smiling, he was also not reaching into his wallet. I'd been partner here now for about six months. I'd been balancing the books. I'd hired an employee who much more than paid for himself. I'd brought in several dozen cases from the publicity I'd earned the firm. I'd even bought furniture for the office. The only way Malcolm would acknowledge the partnership in our day-to-day operations, though, was that he no longer felt it necessary to buy the coffee. Second note for same discussion.

"You should stand up for yourself."

That's what Rafe would say. Or what I thought Rafe would say if Malcolm didn't have him running around the city twenty-four hours a day chasing married cheats and taking nasty skin pix.

"You should tell him to shove it. Get his own coffee." Of course, Rafe wasn't particularly fond of Malcolm lately.

I stood at the counter ordering Malcolm's extra sweet, extra light and the tart's black with Sweet 'n Low. Malcolm would never admit he was doing anything but helping the firm.

"Of course, I knew I was treating you like shit. That's what that kind of woman wants. Attentive men. No competition from other women. I just wanted to get the business for the company. Our company. If I'd known you were so insecure, I would have let the job slide."

"Is that why your eyes were glued so firmly on her cleavage?"

"Of course. I've never seen breasts before, Rita. What do you think?"

Anything for the firm. And what could I say? Business had picked up for a while after the publicity we got a few months back. A few more missing-persons cases, some collections, a little recovery of stolen objects and funds, even one particularly distasteful blackmail case. Most of the cases were handled successfully, though we never did find the newborn stolen from the hospital. None of those cases, however, got us any more publicity. And sooner or later the bread-and-butter work, the divorce cases, wormed their way back to being the focus of the business.

All of which meant that I'd wait to talk to Malcolm about the treatment until after the bimbo left. No reason to scare her off. When the choice was between kissing a little behind and not taking a paycheck for a week, I'd pucker up most every time. Being a partner was a wonderful thing.

"Here's your coffee."

I considered setting it down with just enough force to redecorate that blue dress, but settled for my best nauseating smile instead.

Malcolm must have explained that I was the primary operative in the agency, because right away they began to share her little problem.

"Hannah's having some trouble with her marriage."

The poor guy was lucky to escape with his skin.

"I'm so sorry."

"Actually, we're separated. Malcolm here told me you were divorced."

She held the Styrofoam cup to her lips, leaving a wet red mark on the rim. She made it a point to slowly lick the one drop of coffee that sat on her lip with her tongue.

"He did?"

Malcolm sat there transfixed by her amazing ability to drink coffee.

"It just came up."

"Yes, Malcolm is so understanding."

He understood just how comforting it would be to Hannah to know that I was one rung lower than she was on the marriage ladder. I wondered how long it would be before

I'd found out he'd promised I'd do her floors and windows and drop by mornings to walk the Pekingese I'd bet she owned.

"Her husband . . ."

"Noah Lowell. He's a professor. At Columbia."

She took another sip.

"Hannah feels he might be seeing someone."

I tried not to smile too much. Just enough to make her squirm a little. Still, I couldn't be sure if Malcolm had told her about Frank and all the extracurricular activity he'd availed himself of while we were still married. He'd told her everything else about me. And that would have blown the whole effect. I made do with a small smile.

"I thought you said you were separated. Why shouldn't he be seeing someone? Of course, I'm just playing devil's advocate."

"Of course. There's no reason he shouldn't be seeing someone. It's just that he said he wasn't. And . . . well, this is a little delicate."

The only thing I could think of that could be more delicate than your husband cheating on you would be your husband not cheating on you. All of a sudden, I realized that it was he who wanted a divorce, who'd wanted the separation, and that the only way she could escape any responsibility for the dissolution of the marriage, escape the idea that she hadn't just lost out in a fair competition, that there was actually something lacking in her, was if she could establish that it was all his fault. He couldn't be dissatisfied with her. Therefore, she couldn't believe he wasn't seeing someone. Therefore, he must be lying.

"You want us to find who he's seeing."

"Someone must have done something to him. Maybe they hooked him on drugs or something. He told me he'd tried them in college. He's acting so strange lately."

"Did he say anything or do anything to give you some idea as to who it might be?"

She shook her head and took another sip of coffee.

"This must be hell for you," Malcolm offered. Hannah nodded appreciatively.

We ran through all the usual possibilities. A neighbor. A friend. A colleague. As much as Hannah wanted an out none of them seemed to offer a good candidate.

"You said he was a professor."

"At Columbia."

"Yes. Do you think it might be a student?"

Hannah didn't say anything, but the way her body stiffened answered just as well. For a woman who measured herself on the scale Hannah seemed to use, a younger woman was the greatest threat of all. Her husband's access to all those young bodies probably tormented her. She must have realized what I was thinking.

"It's not as though I haven't had the opportunity to stray myself."

"I'm sure."

"I have a very influential position at Stern's in Jersey."

I nodded.

"I manage cosmetics," she said, pursing her lips together while eyeing my own rather inelaborate use of makeup at the same time. She wasn't ready to stop, and it was still possible that she might say something that would be useful later on.

"I get at least one proposition a week. A serious one a month. And from some very eligible men. There was this one product rep from New Agenda collagen antiaging who . . . well, I don't need to tell you."

Malcolm must have been imagining what she didn't need to tell or else he was wondering how to get into the cosmetic sales business quickly, because he reached into his pocket

for a handkerchief to wipe his upper lip. Hannah looked
over.

"It's a little hot in here, don't you think?" he asked.

Hannah smiled, and touched Malcolm's knee playfully,
causing Malcolm to make a second go-around at that lip of
his. I hated to break up the party.

"How long have you been separated?"

"A couple of months. I gave Malcolm here Noah's address in the city. Our house is in Jersey."

"Is there anything you think I should know?"

Hannah thought.

"Only that I wouldn't limit the list of suspects too quickly.
That man changed. Believe me. I wouldn't be surprised if he
was a homo or something. I've heard about that."

That deep insight having been offered, I launched into my
usual warning that these investigations seldom turn up anything the client didn't already know. Most of the time the
suspicions were true, finding out who the other woman was
did little to solve the basic problems in the marriage, and
things still fell apart, only the client would be out several
hundred dollars.

But while most times when I gave this speech the romantic in me hoped the client wouldn't pursue the investigation,
this time I ran through it on automatic pilot. Hannah Lowell didn't much care about saving her marriage. She just
didn't like being dumped and would feel more comfortable
knowing someone had stolen her husband. Besides, I was
still edgy from last night. I wanted her gone as quickly as
possible. And I still had to have it out with Malcolm after
she left.

"I understand. I'd like to go ahead with the investigation.
I want a name."

She paused.

"And a picture."

I handed her a sheet of paper.

"This is a standard set of questions we've devised to help put together a profile of our subject. It helps expedite the process. Have it back tomorrow, and we can begin."

"Malcolm has already started to help fill it out. I'd like you to begin work immediately."

In the window behind Hannah I could see it was starting to rain.

"Immediately?"

"Yes. Malcolm said he might even have something to report tonight."

"Tonight?"

The level of my conversation was approaching that of Polly the Amazing Parrot of the Dark Continent. I smiled what was probably a remarkably stupid smile.

"Yes. Malcolm was kind enough to ask me to dinner."

I looked over at Malcolm, who was licking his fleshy lips, whether in anticipation of tonight's dinner or tomorrow's clash with me I wasn't sure. What I did know was that staying here much longer would only get me sick.

"Well, then, I guess I'll just let you two finish up the sheet."

Hannah smiled. I looked past her out the window. It was beginning to come down harder. Great. Too wet to go for an early lunch. That meant killing the next half hour or so in the lobby. I shook hands with Hannah, gave Malcolm the dirtiest look I could, and headed out the door. And all the way down the elevator I could hear Malcolm's voice explaining how there was a way you had to treat certain clients, a way at which he'd become a master, and how it wasn't easy having dinner with a cheap tramp on the company expense account, pouring wine down her throat, staring at her cleavage, and doing everything in his power to land this client in his own special way. And at the same time I could hear my own small voice telling me how glad I was that I'd finally become a partner.

FIVE

♦

I stood in the small lobby that used to be shabby and run-down but which now had been covered in a garish mirror decor in hopes of attracting more upscale tenants, looked out the glass door at the rain coming down, and wished I'd thought to bring my coffee along. This wasn't working.

Since making me partner, Malcolm had been backing away from the business even more than he had before. He still went out of his way to meet newly separated women. He kept up his memberships in three different support groups even though his wife had left him more than four and a half years ago. He was a contributing subscriber to four museums. He took two night classes a week at the New School. In human relations. But all that had gotten to be fun for Malcolm. And besides, he probably figured that sooner or later he'd get lucky.

What had changed was that Malcolm no longer participated in the cases. He'd bring them in as best he could. There was always a steady stream of divorce work. And if that ever began to run thin, Malcolm would make a few calls and we'd pick up a few collections, some background checks, maybe even some property-recovery cases. But that's where Malcolm's contribution would end. When it came to actually pursuing cases, Malcolm turned the work over to Rafe and me. If there was some finesse involved, I'd get the case. If it was mostly legwork, the case would go to Rafe. Since divorce is mostly legwork, Rafe took the brunt of the schedule.

Meanwhile, Malcolm would sit back at the office. He'd answer the phone when no one else was there to do it for him. But he wouldn't make calls himself. No investigative work, even of the sedentary variety. I was a partner now, and that made him the senior partner. It wouldn't do to have him shuffling along asking questions or taking nasty photographs. He had a reputation to uphold. He kept his head in the business only enough to know when Rafe and I were getting disgruntled. Then he'd somehow work into a conversation the value of experience and reputation for an agency. How his mere presence attracted more business than the agency's level of competence could achieve. He'd point out how I had yet to bring in anywhere near the volume of clients that he did without even trying. And then he'd sit back, pick up a newspaper, bite down on a Danish, and wait till the next time we got a little fed up having him around.

Suddenly, from out of the rain, Rafe came running across the street. He hadn't brought an umbrella. He probably didn't own one. His only protection was one of those crush-able, powder-blue polyester hats. Leaning against the wall, he looked like some fat kid waiting for his teacher to come. Only he was well over fifty, the kind of guy you saw so often in the city that you never noticed him—his shirt not quite reaching his pants, his ever-present copy of the *Post* tucked under one side of his open jacket. I opened the door to let him in.

"Good morning."

Rafe only nodded back. He might as well have spit in my face. This was the guy who was supposed to be my charm, the guy whose job it was to back me up, save my life, make me smile.

"Malcolm's upstairs with a client. I think he's trying to hustle up more than a case."

Another nod.

"Things okay?"

"Not so good, Rita."

Things hadn't been good for Rafe ever since I'd made partner, which was just about as long as he'd been officially working for us. When I'd been Malcolm's assistant, the old guy had been reluctant to run me around too much. Out-of-town travel cases were discouraged and I rarely got more than two night stakeouts a week. Even though Malcolm prided himself on being a modern man, the assignments probably had something to do with my being a woman, and that was fine with me. Rafe, however, wasn't a woman. And Malcolm didn't seem to like Rafe much. A lack of class, he'd say, doing the pot-and-kettle bit without even a trace of irony. That combination led Malcolm to drive Rafe out of the office as much as possible, so much so that it was already Thursday and this was the first time I'd seen Rafe this week.

"How long are you going to put up with this?" Rafe asked.

It was his standard line of attack. Why should I work with a partner who contributed nothing to the agency, who was offensive to the employee, who took up half the profits and had lousy eating habits? That last part really bothered Rafe. The discussion usually came up after a particularly rough stretch of work.

"You've been working hard?"

Rafe snorted as if that was all the response necessary, but he apparently couldn't resist elaborating.

"Right now I'm working seven divorces, six with pictures, four collections, two character checks, and tomorrow night I'm waitering a bachelor party for a girl who's not ready to trust her daddy's money to her true love until she's sure he's true. I'm too old to be hanging around with a bunch of horny drunks and some beaten-down old stripper."

"Maybe Malcolm would relieve you on that last one."

It was supposed to be a joke, but the look on Rafe's face showed that he didn't take it quite so humorously.

"I haven't spent more than one night at home in the last month, Rita. Peg let me get started in this thing 'cause she knows how much I wanted it, but this is crazy."

"We need more help around here. I'll talk to Malcolm about it."

"I'm not even making any money."

"We're doing okay. Maybe Malcolm will give you a little raise."

"You don't understand."

"What?"

"Rita, Peg's left me."

He wasn't just telling me, he was challenging me. It was his marriage, but he wanted to know what I was going to do about it.

"I'm sorry."

It didn't seem to be enough.

"And instead of chasing after her like I should, like I want to, I'm going to spend the day following some sleazeball executive vice president and watch him push coins into peep shows on his lunch hour."

He wasn't going to let it drop.

"You need some time off. Like I said, I'll talk to Malcolm. I'll see what I can do."

He was about to say something, then thought better of it. He ran his fingers over a plaster cast of an angel on the wall that looked original but had actually been added when the landlord remodeled the lobby.

"I thought you were a partner," he said.

We stood there staring at each other. Something had changed. Rafe was no longer blaming Malcolm. He'd finally figured out that I was his boss, too. And I guess it was just occurring to me that I wasn't going to have the luxury of blaming Malcolm for everything that went wrong around the office any longer. We stared a little while longer till Hannah Lowell came sashaying out of the elevator.

"You can go up now."

She was smiling her smuggest grin as she opened her umbrella and hailed a cab that seemed to materialize out of nowhere.

I followed Rafe to the office, desperate to get my hands on Hannah's information and make my exit. Malcolm was sitting at his desk. Whistling.

SIX

◆

I was thinking about Hannah Lowell and Malcolm's whistling on the subway all the way up to Columbia University. I'd gotten used to his trying with every woman he came in contact with. But I'd always just assumed they all turned him down. Sure, maybe every once in a while he found some particularly pathetic potential divorcee who succumbed to his attentions. I didn't count them and I didn't want to think about it. But Hannah Lowell, as despicable as she might be, was not pathetic. What did he offer her? How much dinner could she eat?

Now, while Rafe was out taking snapshots of a Long Island accountant copping a nooner with the receptionist and Malcolm was smiling smugly with his feet on the desk knowing what Rafe and I must be thinking, I was on my way to check out the cause of Noah Lowell's leaving his supposedly irresistible wife. And while I stared straight ahead, avoiding the spaced-out gaze of the crackhead across from me as the No. 1 train slowly rattled uptown, Malcolm's words played over in my head.

"I did what I had to do and we got the case."

She couldn't. No way.

Columbia University. West and south of Harlem. There it sits. In all the time I'd lived here, I'd only found three reasons to go up there, all of them job-related. Today was no different.

Malcolm had given me the name of a building, college buildings of course having names rather than numbers. It was a brick-and-ivy number that was supposed to contain the work space of the straying husband. Something was wrong. I didn't feel much like playing detective right now, especially in a divorce case. It wasn't Malcolm's game-playing, and I couldn't even say I was sad about Wilsey. But there was work to be done on Wilsey's murder. Work that involved me. So what was I doing here? Aside from making a buck, I couldn't figure it, but maybe a buck was enough.

I adjusted my jacket collar against the thickening mist and made my way through the university's cast-iron gates. Hannah had provided a schedule of the guy's classes so I'd be sure to catch him in. That was important. I didn't know much about higher education, but one thing I'd learned.

Professors, in general, do their best to avoid their workplace as much as possible.

Inside, the building looked like an old high school. Drab glossy paint. Old linoleum. Clocks on every wall. Gave me the willies. I took the elevator to the fifth floor and proceeded to ask the buxom, washed-out, black-haired, black eye-linered student secretary at the front desk what room Noah Lowell was teaching in. She put down her stub of a cigarette, smiled as if she'd been told she'd be fired if she didn't, and pointed down the hall.

The first classroom I came to was large and filled to overflowing. Inside, students dressed in New York fashion statements ranging from proletarian custodial to the ever-popular all-black uniform listened in rapt attention to some suntanned blond guy with a paid-for smile whose name I should have known but didn't. I stood at the door and listened long enough to hear the room break out laughing at a joke that wasn't funny. For some reason I got the feeling this course wasn't Problems in Contemporary Film Theory and moved on.

I hadn't quite figured just how I was going to observe Noah Lowell in action. I'd only had the subway ride up here to think about it and I'd blown that thinking about Malcolm. This whole job was beginning to take on the character of my favorite anxiety dream—walking into a test when I hadn't taken the class, didn't recognize the material, and the grade really mattered.

I stopped just outside the next room—a much smaller one, with most seats empty. No one was speaking. Lowell's wife suspected that whatever was going on was going on at Columbia. Okay, so here I was. But until I got here, I hadn't realized just how tricky it was to observe someone completely unnoticed in a school. Where was I supposed to hide? In a corner of the classroom? Under a desk? Alone in the hall with a sign stapled to my forehead saying "Don't Notice Me, I'm Inconspicuous"?

"Can I help you?"

Standing in front of me was a tall, sharp-featured guy with a distance runner's physique, gray-flecked curly hair edging toward the long side, and black horn-rims, who fit Hannah Lowell's description of her husband uncomfortably well. Only cuter. Academic-looking type. Coming of age during the war. Staying in school just as long as he could. Slightly mismatched clothes, mostly in the corduroy and tweed family, all of them rumpled. Not killer looks, but they worked for me and that usually meant they could work for someone else. Not that appearances had all that much to do with fidelity. I noticed he also had that eye-contact bit professors do down pat, which could be something of a turn-on in the right context. I answered in the only way I could think of.

"What?"

"You're not a student, are you?"

So much for the myth of maintaining my girlish youth. Still, he was neither friendly nor rude, not coming on to me no matter how much his wife would have wanted to interpret his questions as such. I figured he wouldn't call security, but there was no reason to take any chances. I smiled. And lied.

"I'm a prospective student."

He looked me up and down, again not really checking me out in any way I was used to being checked out, then nodded back at the classroom with the suntan in it.

"Screenplay Construction is in Room 511," he said, more with resignation than disdain.

I wasn't feeling much like a detective right now, having already made contact with a subject I was only supposed to observe. But even with whatever minimal skills I might have, I could tell film theory was not the big draw here. How could they attract students to take academic courses when right in the same department there were professors who had the potential to turn those students into screenwriters, directors, and stars? Hell, if I weren't getting paid to be here, I'd be checking out the guy with the suntan myself.

I'd blown the anonymity thing, so Rafe would have to pick up the surveillance angle. That would teach him to ask me to lighten his workload. In the meantime, I'd do what I could to check out Noah Lowell more directly. That meant another lie.

"Actually, I wanted to look into the more theoretical side of film."

Lowell looked surprised, then shrugged and invited me into his class. I was gambling he wouldn't ask me any more on the subject. I'd never been much on school to begin with, and calling them films instead of movies was all I could pull out of my hat in the theory department.

I took a seat in the back of the class and looked around. Hell, his wife had nothing to worry about up here. There were only two women in the class. One weighed in at a good two hundred and fifty pounds, wore a crew cut, work boots, and a Gertrude Stein sweatshirt and the other, unless she was putting on an act, looked like she'd much rather be sitting in the class down the hall.

Lowell walked to the desk at the front of the class and resumed his lecture. He was talking about the hidden agenda of some author whose name must have come up before the break.

I looked at my watch. The class had forty-five minutes to run. Lowell was just building momentum.

"Why does Metz introduce scopophilia to the film experience?"

"How does it open up the film experience?"

"Does it open up the film experience?"

He wasn't going to get an answer from me, which was only natural. But he wasn't going to get an answer from anyone else in the class either. Of the five sitting in the seats, one had his head on his desk, two others held theirs in their hands, and a fourth leaned back so far in her chair that her failure to fall challenged every known law of gravity.

I tried to picture the guy with Hannah. He seemed so much looser than she was. Interested in the kinds of things I couldn't imagine her having anything to do with. Things like thinking, for example. It was like those "what's wrong with this picture" games I played as a kid.

Just then a sixth student entered the room and headed for a desk with some books already sitting on it. She was tall and well dressed. Tailored skirt. Silk shirt. Her hair was pulled back. She wore glasses. Almost the perfect image of the woman who would easily be transformed into a raving beauty if she just let herself. And the way she looked at Lowell had nothing to do with Marx or scopophilia or whatever else Lowell was talking about except maybe Freud.

I broke out the notebook and began to take notes. This might well be the woman Hannah Lowell was worried about. A younger, more educated, more tasteful version of herself. From the muscles in her arm I could tell she worked out. She was perfect.

But Lowell did nothing to play to her. He wasn't avoiding her, but he wasn't playing to her. She was hanging on his every word, but he paid no more attention to her than to the others. He was either trying to fake out the rest of the class, disguising this torrid affair as best he could, or he really didn't give a damn for the girl.

Gertrude Stein and two others left before the class even ended. Two more put on their coats while Lowell was still talking. Lowell ignored them, finished his lecture, then placed his notes back in a folder on the desk in front of him.

Perfection got up from her desk, looked my way, then said something in a low voice to Lowell.

"What?"

He was making her speak up, destroying whatever intimacy she wanted to create. Was he still trying to cover up, or was he just trying to avoid falling into her clutches? Tough call.

Perfection asked something about an assignment and special help. Lowell told her to make an appointment with the department secretary. Perfection left the room, at least seemingly, in defeat.

"Thanks for letting me sit in."

Lowell turned, surprised there was someone still in the room.

"You liked it?"

He stood there, suddenly fully focused on me, the eye thing, only in the wrong context as far as I was concerned. It was like being back at school: "Rita, how would you respond to Gandhi's flagrant violations of the law if you wanted to keep India under your control? Rita?"

Only he wasn't intimidating, more like a new kid on the block who finally found someone willing to play with his new football.

"It was a little over my head."

"Interesting."

He was waiting for me to say something more.

"But I liked it."

It wasn't much, but it was all I had to offer. When he smiled, I was glad I'd said it. I was also glad he waited for me to get up before turning and leaving. I was glad we rode down in the elevator together. I was even glad I hadn't brought an umbrella so he could offer to walk me to the subway and I could accept.

"You're not going to go to school here, are you?"

"Probably not."

"Interesting."

"It's not your fault."

"No. Of course not. It was nice meeting you."

And before I knew it, I was saying something I wasn't glad to be saying right then and that I'd be even less glad to have said later.

"Maybe we could have lunch sometime."

"Huh?"

"I'm sorry. I don't know why I said that."

"No. That's okay. I was just surprised. Are you sure you're not going to be a student here?"

I laughed.

Lowell shrugged, told me where he lived and that his number was listed. After that, he left. I walked down the stairs to the subway. I'd just asked the husband of a client out on a date.

"Yes, Hannah, I'm sorry, your husband is seeing somebody."

"Who is the bitch? I'll rip her face off."

"Hannah, that's, uh, the tricky part."

It would never wash. I decided to call Malcolm and burn off the rest of the day. I'd blown this case. We'd have to turn it over to Rafe. I wouldn't call Lowell, of course. That would be crazy. I'd drop it, let it lie, go home and have a couple of beers, take a nap, and maybe when I woke up I'd be a professional investigator again.

I stepped around a drunken woman with some kind of European accent mumbling about the goddamned Bulgarians and called Malcolm on the pay phone.

"Rita, I told you not to worry. The police called. They made an arrest."

SEVEN

♦

Jesus Rantz was sitting on Morris's desk when I walked into the detectives' room for the second time that day. He never looked up to see me. It just worked out that he got up to leave just as I got there.

"Sugar, you should have called. Here you come all this way to do the wild thing with me and I've got to run. See if Lenny can hold you till I get back."

I hoped that not responding would minimize my contact with the guy. He still couldn't resist sticking out his tongue and wiggling it around in the air a couple of times. It was the type of thing I'd come to expect since I'd divorced a cop.

"What can I do for you, Rita?"

Lenny was smiling like a cop who'd solved an unsolvable murder in less than twenty-four hours. On his desk was a cup of coffee and a half-eaten cinnamon roll that Rantz had been blocking from my view.

"Sorry to interrupt your breakfast. Do you mind talking?"

"No problem. Want some coffee?"

I shook my head.

"What's the story?"

"No story. We caught the guy who iced Wilsey."

"Who was it?"

Morris opened his desk and flipped me a photograph. Hispanic-looking kid. Late twenties, maybe. Short. Nasty-looking, but that didn't mean much. Mother Teresa would look nasty in a mug shot. I'd never seen him before.

"His name's Sarmiento. Bobby Sarmiento."

"Never heard of him."

"He was Wilsey's partner."

"Some partner."

"Yeah. The kid's a junkie, too. They'd been busted together over the last couple of years every time they'd been busted. Breaking and entering, mostly. Some nickel-and-dime dealing. All the usual."

"Any violence?" I wasn't sure if I was asking about Sarmiento or Wilsey.

"There is now." Morris laughed.

"Did he confess?"

Lenny just smirked. Confessions, especially to murder, were not all that easy to come by.

"We figure when Wilsey came by the other night, he didn't think you'd be home. When you were, what the heck, he'd drop by, say hello, and see what you owned. He comes back the next day with his buddy. This time you're not there. They break in. Get in a fight. Maybe they're a little high or something. One thing leads to another. Wilsey gets waxed."

It didn't make much sense to me. Why would they get in a fight while burglarizing my apartment? There wasn't much to fight over. Moreover, why would Wilsey come back to rip me off after he'd seen the pitiful collection of possessions my apartment contained? Still, that didn't mean it couldn't happen.

Lenny was so pleased with himself, I figured I wouldn't mention any of that stuff and ruin the afterglow of that cinnamon roll. And the case was closed in such a way that it really didn't have much to do with me. Wilsey'd probably wanted to stick it to Frank. If he still cared about stuff like that. He really only wanted some money. My professional standing wouldn't be helped any by not solving the case myself. But considering how quickly the whole thing got taken care of, it wouldn't hurt much either. It was so neat and perfect, I half-expected the sun to be shining when I got outside.

So why did I hear myself asking Lenny Morris for a copy of Wilsey's arrest report?

"Why do you want that?"

He didn't have to give it to me. But that wouldn't stop me from getting it. He knew that. It was public information. And with the Freedom of Information Act, these things were pretty easy to get ahold of nowadays. Of course, that didn't mean Morris had to like it.

"He was a friend a long time ago. I've got a pretty good idea what became of him. I guess I just want to know it all."

It was the sincere approach, made even easier since it wasn't all that far from the truth. Even better, it appealed to the nice-guy thing Lenny Morris worked at to make his job run smoothly.

"Yeah. Sure. I understand. Here, you want a copy of Sarmiento's while I'm at it?"

I shrugged "Why not" and the big guy lumbered over to a tired old copy machine and did the required work.

"Here."

"Thanks."

"We'll be in touch if the thing goes to court and the D.A. needs you to testify."

"I won't be much help."

"You know what they say about every little bit."

"Thanks for taking care of this so quickly."

"Hey. He was a cop."

EIGHT

♦

Malcolm was alone in the office when I got there. It was almost closing time and he was still whistling. Poor guy. What he was expecting from this date could only let him down.

"Rita. Thank God. What did you find out?"

"The cops think Wilsey was killed by his burglary partner. A kid named Sarmiento."

"Not about that. About Lowell. Did you find anything? Is he boffing the babes up there or what?"

I'd almost forgotten this morning's disastrous encounter at Columbia. Which wasn't entirely bad. Especially that little part where I'd asked Noah Lowell out to lunch.

"I don't think so."

"What? One trip up to Columbia and you're so sure he's clean?"

"I didn't say I was sure. I said I think he's keeping himself clean, at least as far as his students go."

"And how do you know that?"

The old man was desperate. He wanted something on Lowell. If not proof, at least suspicion. Something with which to make an impression on Hannah Lowell. Something that might keep her emotionally off balance. Something to help him score tonight.

I could have answered that he wouldn't go out with me until I'd told him I wouldn't take his class, which would also mean he probably wasn't all that seriously seeing anyone else either. However, the truth was only one of several avenues to take.

"Malcolm, you hired me and trained me. You told me to develop my hunches and you have a pretty good idea of how those hunches pan out. I don't think he's seeing anyone."

Malcolm stopped whistling. His whole body started to sag. The light went out of his eye. I couldn't do it to the guy. At least let it be Hannah who burst his bubble.

"Okay. I don't think this is important, and I don't think he had any interest in her, but there was this one woman in the class who looked hot for the guy."

Two if you counted me, I supposed. But there was no time to enjoy my little irony. The blackout was over. Malcolm's lights came back on with a vengeance.

"Who was she? You get a name? A description?"

"Not yet on the name. But she's attractive. Slick dresser. Especially for the campus crowd. I mean, if he was going to be interested in someone, she'd be someone he could get interested in, I suppose."

"She's our girl. I know it. Rita. You're beautiful. Tell me you're planning on following her. Getting a name. This is a major lead. I know it. I know it."

He straightened his tie in an imaginary mirror.

"You don't mind locking up, do you?"

He was out the door before I'd even had time to answer. If I wasn't so sure he'd be hell to live with in the morning, I might have even cracked a smile.

There was no reason to wait around the office. Rafe wouldn't be stopping by. He was out checking to see if a teller's wife was skipping her bowling league to wiggle under the next-door neighbor. The damp weather had gotten to me and I was too cold to go grab a beer. And somehow I still wasn't too keen on spending a lot of time alone in my apartment.

I wasn't sure just what usually happened when we weren't at the office. We had the message machine, of course, but mostly the callers hung up without speaking. If tonight was anything to judge by, though, the place must normally be jumping.

The first call was from a guy named Henry Mencia. He'd just read about Wilsey in the paper. He said he was a headhunter and wanted to meet me about a possible opening in a corporate security position he thought might be very attractive to me. I told him I didn't have much experience with the high-tech end of the business, but he was convinced with recent events being what they were, I could make it on the tough-girl image. So much for a murder being detrimental to my career. He gave me his number and told me to think it over.

The phone hadn't sat in the cradle for more than a second when a slight, short Hispanic woman knocked on the door. There was no New York attitude. She looked old. Her skin was leathered and wrinkled. Even in the cold and rain, she wore only a thin cotton dress.

She looked at me with some suspicion for a moment, then stuck a piece of paper in my hand. On it were written my name and the agency's address. She was looking for me, I figured, and I gave her a nod to let her know she'd found me.

I led her inside, sat back down at my desk, and pointed her toward the guest chair. Only the woman wouldn't sit.

"Rosa Sarmiento."

She said it as though that explained why she was here and it pretty much did. Unfortunately, there was something in the way she pronounced the name that made it unnecessary for her to explain she spoke no English. I nodded. This didn't promise to be easy. I'd dropped Spanish some time early in high school and the only things that stuck in my head were useful things like all the curse words and that *albóndigas* was the word for meatballs.

"My husband. . ."

My heart just about stopped right there. The little woman whom I'd thought was Bobby Sarmiento's mother was his wife. His wife, for God's sake. That only left two possibilities. Either the kid had married an old woman or the old woman in front of me was only twenty-six. I made a mental note to stop at the "Y" on the way home tonight.

"Bobby Sarmiento?"

She nodded.

"He is . . . in jail. He say murder. But no."

Between her broken English and the little Spanish I began to recall, the conversation took a good three-quarters of an hour to put together. As far as I could figure it, Bobby Sarmiento was innocent. She conceded he'd worked with Wilsey. She conceded he had a drug habit, a criminal record, and had served time. After all the concessions I was surprised the woman looked as young as she did.

But violence was not one of Sarmiento's vices. He would never kill anyone. Even high. Besides, he was with her the night Wilsey got killed. She'd told this to the police when they took Bobby away. She'd told it to Rantz and Morris when she went over to the precinct to see what she could do. Only no one believed her or cared or anything else. Somebody over there must have given her my name, explaining that I was a detective and the murder happened in my place. Probably Rantz.

She wanted me to get her husband out of jail. He was innocent. I was a detective. She wanted me to find who did it so she could get on with her life. Of course, she didn't have any money. And my Spanish would never be good enough to explain how private investigators work for fees, especially if she'd made up her mind not to understand.

I took down as much of her story as I was sure I got right, then got her address, since she didn't have a phone. But that was it. There were no promises made. I believed Rosa Sarmiento just as much as the cops did. Everybody was innocent. And just because her husband had never been caught for killing anyone before didn't mean there wasn't a first time.

She looked at me cold and hard like she'd probably looked at Rantz and Morris. Somewhere under her breath she was probably muttering the same curses that she'd placed on them. Then, walking with as much of a burden as she could, she trudged slowly out the door.

I'd gotten used to saying no to prospective clients over the years. And the guilt button she'd tried to push had long since quit functioning. I owed Rosa Sarmiento nothing. And even if I did, it wasn't enough to make me explain to Malcolm that I was taking on a case for no money.

But the murder had occurred in my apartment. And for whatever reason, I still wasn't convinced of the scenario Morris painted back at the precinct. I picked up the arrest reports on Wilsey and Sarmiento and began to leaf through them. Just a little light reading, really. And just because I wasn't taking on the case, it wouldn't kill me to stop by Wilsey's apartment tomorrow on my way to work.

NINE

♦

I didn't find anything particularly interesting in Wilsey's arrest report. Morris was right. Mostly breaking and entering. Possession of stolen property. Possession of narcotics, sometimes with intent to sell. It was steady, too. For at least the last six years. No fits and starts. If he'd held a job during any of this time, it hadn't kept him out of trouble. Most depressing of all, except for a couple of arrests up in Bronxville, Wilsey's busts came in primarily lousy neighborhoods. He didn't even have the ambition to break into the kinds of places where he might see a little return for his risk.

He was on a slide. His murder began to seem not only likely, but inevitable. It was just the scenario that still bugged me. Not the Sarmiento part. Sarmiento's record was just about a perfect match of Wilsey's. And for someone who'd never exhibited a tendency toward violence, Rosa Sarmiento would have to explain why he'd been found with a knife more than half the times he'd been caught.

It was the burglary that bothered me. Why my apartment? What were they looking for? Why did he stop by to see me? Why had he brought a present? What was that whole scene about Frank? There was no reason any of it had to make sense, not in the condition Wilsey was in. But the arrest reports hadn't allowed me much of a night's sleep, and going to check the story out looked like as good a way as any to settle my doubts.

When I first moved to the city, the Lower East Side was

one entity, one lousy neighborhood where even students wouldn't venture. But as housing got tighter and punks and clubs began to take their chances with chancy neighborhoods, that lousy neighborhood began to shrink. First the East Village began to expand eastward. Then Chinatown began to press north. Soho began to stretch all the way to Little Italy. The whole Delancey Street Jewish section began to upgrade. And the realtors just invented Noho, an area full of junkies, winos, Hell's Angels, and sweatshops that of course was a natural to be the next luxury area for development. Five years ago you couldn't have paid me to live in any of these places. Now I was kicking myself for the deals I had passed up.

But there was still a Lower East Side. A nasty Lower East Side. A Lower East Side mostly unserviced by public transportation for the simple reason that no one with the power to direct a bus or train line could think of any possible reason why anyone would want to go there. Places where the disappearance of a working-class white girl like myself would elicit more comments about what she was doing there than about how terrible and tragic the whole thing was. It was the one part of the city where a guy like Wilsey could still afford to live.

Finding where he lived wasn't too difficult. I needed no skip-tracing tactics like tracking down his mother, his driver's license, or an old friend. The guy had a phone. The phone was listed. Some times things just fall your way. It was so easy, I would have felt stupid that I didn't know he lived here except in the nine years since I'd last seen him, I'd never had any reason to call.

Wilsey's building was a good ten blocks from the nearest subway stop. The rain had subsided to a light drizzle. No reason even to wear a jacket. Not once along the way did anyone turn to stare at me. It was the way they didn't look that made me feel uncomfortable. Like they were only using the sides of their eyes. Like they wouldn't want anyone to know they were watching. That left it up to me to imagine why. That kind of imagining I found myself pretty good at.

Wilsey's block was like every other one I'd passed since I'd started walking. One empty lot. A couple of abandoned buildings. Outside his building, one of the bums from the Bowery seemed to have wandered over and set up camp. He was a heavy-set guy who probably once had some muscles, but now was just a sickening mass of flab. His skin was that pasty pink-white you could only achieve through years of severe alcohol abuse coupled with malnutrition and a lack of medical care. A thick layer of dirt on his clothes and an even thicker stench made the picture complete. As I walked past him into the building, he tipped his threadbare, sweat-stained cowboy hat to me, exposing some mangy white hair beneath. At least someone would know where I'd gone. Big relief.

Inside, the stench was just about the same as out. The same evil sayings that were written on the outside of the buildings were written on the walls inside. It was just darker. And damper. And the air didn't move. I pulled at my jacket as if it were still raining.

Wilsey's apartment was a couple of flights up. The door was locked. There was no police sticker on the door, so either they hadn't been here yet or they weren't that interested in keeping anybody out. I knocked. There was no answer. The building was old. The doors were solid and couldn't be forced. I thought about jimmying the lock, but there were easier ways to do things and the last thing I needed right now was to get busted for breaking and entering. Especially in this apartment.

A skinny little weasellike like man with greased-back hair and a gold tooth watched me from one flight up. He wasn't the type to call the cops. But I wasn't going to push it. I knocked one last time, shrugged my shoulders, gave a frustrated smile to the weasel and headed back downstairs.

The cowboy was still sitting outside stinking when I got there. There was no one else to ask, so I figured what the heck.

"You stay around here a lot?"

The cowboy nodded.

"Is there a super in the building?"

He took a good look at me, rubbing his hand across his stubbled face, then spoke in an unnaturally high, pure voice.

"You're a Scorpio."

Astrology was something that always bugged me. People guessing my sign like they knew more about me than I did myself. It was especially annoying when people guessed right. I nodded.

"Is there a super?"

"It's aggressive. That Scorpio. Sexy. Yeah."

"Is there a super?"

"You get a lot of suicides though."

That was enough. I figured I'd take my chances knocking on doors inside. There'd be at least a fifty-fifty shot I'd be able to leave alive.

"One-C."

It was the cowboy again.

"What?"

"And her name is Bina. And she hits me."

It had started raining a little harder. The cowboy didn't look like he even had a thought of getting shelter inside. If it was raining, he'd get wet. I knew if I gave him money he'd just blow it on booze and it would make it that much harder for him to leave this hole, but the guy might have saved my life, and it just wasn't my place to tell him how to spend the ten bucks I dropped in his lap.

I got to 1-C and knocked. The name on the door said Kryczyvyk. Inside, I could hear a kid screaming. And someone swearing.

"What?"

A woman shouted through the door.

"Are you Bina?"

"What do you want?"

"I want to look in Wilsey Weiss's apartment. I left something there and I need to get it back."

I didn't know if the news of his death had traveled back here yet, but I sure didn't want to tell her Wilsey told me to meet him here and get caught in a lie my first sentence.

"What do you want me to do?"

"I was hoping you could let me in."

There was a silence on the other side of the door.

"How much?"

"Twenty."

"Fifty."

For a freebie, it was already costing me plenty. I said okay and the door opened. Bina turned out to be a hard, skinny little woman, with greasy hair, wearing a Harley-Davidson T-shirt and the kind of jeans designers never put their names on. Long dark hair ran the full length of her bony arms. The screaming kid was a skeevy-looking thing who appeared to be a lot older than he sounded. She gave a dirty look. I handed her the money.

"How'd you find me?"

There was no reason to reveal my source and have him catch more hell than he already had. I shrugged.

"Fucking cowboy. All right, babe, let's go."

She headed up the stairs, half-dragging the kid along with her.

"I let you in there and I leave, okay? You take something, I don't want to know about it. I didn't do this, right, babe?"

She got to Wilsey's door and started to unlock it when she

looked up and saw the sleazeball, who was still standing at the top of the next flight.

"What the fuck are you looking at, cocksucker? I told you to get out, didn't I? I'll blow your fucking head off, I see you around here again."

I was about to smile uncomfortably when I saw Bina pull a small-caliber handgun from the waistband of her pants and aim it up the stairs. The sleaze ambled off before she could fire.

"Fucking junkies, turn this place into a goddamned shooting gallery," she muttered under her breath as she opened the door. "There you go, babe. Remember, I don't know nothing about nothing."

I gave her my card and told her to give me a call if she saw anyone in here. Then she left. I didn't have much hope of getting a call, and I wasn't all that eager to come back if I did, but that didn't stop me from wrapping a twenty around the card. The universal language. Besides, who knew the kind of business I might drum up with the circle she traveled in.

Wilsey's apartment was as much a mess as his life had been. And not just cluttered either. The one window was so dirty that little light could penetrate it. There were gaping holes where plaster had fallen off the wall. And wherever the plaster had fallen, there it had stayed. It would have been so much nicer if he'd just died nine years ago, if the last nine years hadn't happened, if I didn't have to think about them. I wasn't thinking about all the things he might have done, the things he might have been involved in that would make him live in a place like this. It was just nine years in this hole.

The apartment was a one-room studio. No kitchen. Just a double burner and a small refrigerator. The remains of whatever had boiled over on the burner over the years had solidified, caked, like they'd been frozen in stop motion running down the side and no one ever bothered turning the projector back on. Crumbs, marijuana seeds, and rat feces competed for room on the cracked Formica counter.

I opened a cupboard. Three boxes of Uncle Ben's and a couple of cans of tomato sauce. A half-empty bottle of tequila. In the sink he used as a garbage can were a couple of wrappers for some sweet spongy cupcake thing that looked like it had had pink frosting. Three beers stood alone in the refrigerator. Awful stuff, but still no reason to kill the guy.

The bathroom provided nothing better. More cracked porcelain. More dirt. A shower that looked like he used it to clean horses. A two-hundred-year-old toothbrush missing at least half the bristles it ever had. The medicine cabinet was empty at least of any of the usual niceties. There was an oversized Ziploc plastic bag filled with at least a half a pound of marijuana. Not enough to indicate he was seriously selling. At least not enough to provoke murder.

Back to the main room. Wilsey's mattress was on the floor. The sheets were messed this way and that with so many cigarette burns they appeared to have a designer pattern. Down at one end there was actually charring from some kind of fire. It had been quite a while since they'd been washed, if indeed they ever had.

There was no other furniture. No closets. The few clothes he had were piled in a heap on the floor. This was a man who used to come to my house, eat at my table. He'd been a friend. I tried to remind myself that maybe he was lucky, that the cowboy on the street couldn't afford to live here. It didn't help. I set to work on the clothes.

The search wasn't wholly unproductive. Looking through his pockets, I came up with a dark chunk of material I couldn't identify, but the smell and the fact that it was wrapped in foil suggested it was some sort of narcotic. There were several capsules that corresponded to none of the usual street drugs I was familiar with. They might have even been legit. At the same time, it didn't seem likely that Wilsey was using some sort of generic cold remedy.

It wasn't all that big a find. Unless I was following behind the cops. What I'd found wasn't in any secret stash or hidden under any floorboard. If the cops had left the stuff here, it was because it didn't interest them. I pocketed the drugs.

Aside from that, all I found was an old photograph and an appointment card from a Dr. Henry Brotell, a dentist. Wilsey must have been due for a cleaning when he'd gotten iced. It wasn't so strange to think that Wilsey was taking care of his teeth. The last I'd seen, they looked like they'd needed it. What was strange was that he didn't use some sort of clinic. The photograph, of course, was of him and Frank. It was the only thing in the entire pile of clothes that looked like it had ever seen the inside of a washing machine.

The geek was back at the top of the stairs as I shut the door. It was all a little too much decay for one day. I was glad to get out of there. Glad to see the rain again. Even glad to see the cowboy. He was sitting in the same spot, only he must have moved because now he was drinking a bottle of Mad Dog. So much for helping the unfortunate. The cowboy looked up and tipped his hat as I walked past.

"Remember to watch out for suicide."

TEN

◆

I'd just spent eighty bucks to find out nothing but that Wilsey had drugs in his apartment and the cops were being somewhat lax in this case unless they'd known all along who'd done it. Two things I did know, though. Malcolm would most likely be in a major depression, so I wanted to stay away from the office, and I'd have to keep checking on the Wilsey situation if I wanted to get my money's worth.

I knew that meant I'd have to call on Frank. I'd have to tell him what happened to Wilsey and where it happened. I'd have to find out what he knew about it, if Wilsey had been in touch with him anytime recently, and what he could tell me about way back when. For all I knew, Wilsey could have come looking for Frank. I doubted it.

I would have loved to handle the whole thing with a phone call, or, better yet, a letter, but I knew I'd go see him, even if the idea of the visit made Malcolm's depression seem suddenly more appealing. It was my own form of masochism. Still, I wasn't above postponing the inevitable a little. And the only justification I could come up with at the moment was a trip to the dentist.

Brotell's office was on a quiet tree-lined street in the Twenties off Second Avenue. Under any circumstances the office would have been luxurious. After my trip to the Lower East Side the place was a positive dream. Occupying the first floor of a brownstone, it had none of the usual sterility of the dentists' offices I'd seen. The walls were a rich cream color with light gray trim, like in one of those Colonial houses parents dragged their kids through on second-rate summer vacations. Instead of some functional central fixture, the room was quietly lit with table and floor lamps. Instead of some boxy institutional furniture, the chairs were all Early American. I knew it was special when I saw that the magazines were current and heard jazz over the speakers instead of Muzak. It was like being invited over to some tasteful friend's house for tea, cake, and maybe a little bridgework.

On the way over I'd considered how to approach Brotell. The temptation as an investigator was to fake being a patient. Call up, get an appointment, then ask him my questions with a mouthful of cotton. Scams like that had the advantage of making me feel superior to whomever I was talking to, but the approach had its limitations. Aside from the difficulty of carrying on an interrogation without using my tongue, just in case Sarmiento was innocent, I couldn't help imagining myself having stumbled onto Wilsey's killer only to find myself flat on my back with the guy's drill in my mouth. Besides, from the look of that waiting room, I'd be lucky to get an appointment sometime next month.

I decided to opt for the direct approach and walked up to the receptionist. The guy's hair was blond, close-cropped, and neat. His mustache was trim and just as neat. In keeping with the low-key surroundings, he wore no white lab smock. Instead, he came to work in a short-sleeved shirt and tight-fitting blue jeans.

I took a second look and realized just about anything he would ever wear would be tight-fitting. The guy had muscles everywhere. His neck was the size of my thigh on a bad day. His biceps were the size of my waist. He so dwarfed the ballpoint in his hand that he looked like he might have trouble using it.

"Hello. Can I help you?"

The big guy spoke politely, even friendlily, with a high whiny voice that only matched his body if you had a lot of preconceptions about the psychological makeup of the average muscle boy. He smiled blandly like a potential cousin at some huge family reunion. I hated to nip the relationship in the bud, but I handed him my card.

"I'd like to see Dr. Brotell."

I watched as he studied the card, trying to decide upon the right thing to do.

"Can I tell him what this is in reference to," he whispered, attempting a tone of sincere confidentiality.

I raised my voice half a notch in response, keeping in mind that the waiting room was full of patients.

"Dr. Brotell's name came up in a particularly unpleasant investigation in which our office is taking part. We were hoping to help him avoid any unnecessary embarrassment."

Embarrassment spurred the large guardian to action. Afraid I might raise my voice even louder to respond to further questions, he told me to have a seat and he'd see what he could do.

I hadn't taken much notice of the patients when I first came in, but they certainly fit in with the rest of the office. There was an older woman with short silver hair and a muted red cashmere cowl-neck sweater who was reading the latest issue of *Town & Country*. Next to her was a mother and two too-perfectly behaved children, all with the same white-blond hair, who looked like they'd just come from the off-season party at the yacht club. Two businessmen, one old, one young, sat across the room from each other. A heavily tanned middle-aged dyed blonde with lots of gold, dressed in tennis whites, and with arm muscles that looked like she could put an ace through her opponent's skull, occupied a straight-backed stuffed chair that looked like it had antique value. They all looked wealthy, but that was to be expected.

The only problem was figuring how Wilsey fit in here. I could just see him flopping down next to the semialbino mom on the couch. What was he wearing the last time I saw him? Dirty custodian's pants. Stained sneakers. A dark-colored T-shirt with holes under a flannel shirt of a now indiscernible pattern. Yeah, he'd fit right in.

"Ms. Noonan."

I hadn't realized I expected much in the way of Brotell's looks until he appeared and looked nothing like I expected. For one thing, he was short. Not short like a little under average, but really short. Short for a woman. Right around five feet short. The baby face, even with a mustache and beard, didn't help, and wearing the white jacket only made him look like a kid playing doctor. I half-expected to see a plastic stethoscope around his neck. Even so, he was a match for the receptionist in the muscle department. Every inch of him bulged. There were just fewer inches in which to do the bulging. It was like he'd started out to compensate for his lack of height and then just went a little crazy. I tried not to stare. It wouldn't help to alienate the man before I even opened my mouth.

I got up. The other patients eyed me with scorn, the late intruder who'd somehow jumped the line.

"Dr. Brotell, this will just take a minute."

He made no response. He just turned and walked back into the office area, his stubby legs pushing against each other because of his overly developed thighs.

If Brotell's waiting room was homey, the office he took me to retained the familiar look of a dentist's office. The standard linoleum floor. The usual diplomas on the wall. And, of course, the reclining chair with all the torture devices attached to it. Only a trophy and a framed black-and-white photograph of himself standing on a stage, pumped up, lathered in oil, and wearing a bikini bathing suit, broke the mood. I entered the room, staking out a position as far from the chair as I could. Brotell shut the door behind us.

"Ms. Noonan, I'm a busy man and these are my working hours. I would have appreciated your calling to make an appointment."

The voice was a little too deep, like he was on the phone pretending to be his father excusing himself from school. He put his hands on his hips trying to assert as much authority as possible.

"I apologize for any inconvenience, Dr. Brotell. Do you know a William 'Wilsey' Weiss?"

Brotell looked like he was trying to think through a mental file of all his acquaintances. He paused just long enough to make it appear as though he'd really given it his best shot, then shook his head.

"I'm sorry, Ms. Noonan. The name's not familiar to me. Of course, I know several Weisses, but no Williams or Wilseys. Now if you'll excuse me."

He started to open the door with the purpose of holding it for me to walk through.

"It's just that we found your card in his apartment."

It always sounded better to use "we" in these situations, like there was some swarm of investigators working on the case. It was my own version of Brotell's hands on his hips.

"My card?"

"Yes. You've probably just forgotten him, but we wanted to make sure, you understand."

It was too early to try to corner the guy. I didn't even know what I was looking for.

"Of course. It's also possible he just found the card. My patients are always losing their cards."

He laughed as if to say, "Those darn patients." The laugh

was forced. I handed him the card. It was an appointment written out to William Weiss. It wouldn't hurt to corner the guy just a little.

"Weiss. Weiss. You know what I'll bet this is?"

I didn't respond. He seemed ready to come up with something all on his own.

"I do some pro bono work. You know, poor people, the homeless, all that. I believe you've got to give a little back. My grandfather got his start on a pushcart down on the Lower East Side, you know. Once a month I go down to this clinic and do what I can. Unfortunately, I can't remember the names of all those patients, but . . . Weiss. Weiss. Sure. That must be it."

I noticed his little hand had picked up one of those sharp stainless-steel picks and started poking the end of it into his thumb. The look on his face made me think he'd much prefer to dig it into my gums.

"The appointment is for this office."

You could only keep these things civil for so long.

"He must have had some problem I couldn't handle in just one visit, then, didn't he? What's all this about, Ms. Noonan? And what's it got to do with me?"

"Wilsey's dead. He was shot in the head."

The point of the pick pressed even more forcefully into the little thumb.

"Let me get this straight. Some bum on the Lower East Side gets murdered, and you come looking for his dentist."

Put like that, it did sound a little shaky.

"He had your card."

Brotell took a step forward, forcing me to look even further down than I already was.

"Well, that just about seals it, then, doesn't it? He had my card? I must have murdered him. I saw his teeth, noticed he didn't floss, and couldn't help myself. Ms. Noonan, I've got a waiting room full of patients who need my attention. I'm sorry about your Mr. Weiss. I wish I could help you. But if I don't spend some time on my patients, I won't be able to afford my monthly visit downtown and I'm sure you don't want to be responsible for that. I invite you to leave, Ms. Noonan. And if you decide to return, be prepared to hear from my lawyer."

This time he did hold the door open. And this time I had no ace up my sleeve to hit him with like the card bit I'd used earlier. Still, that lawyer threat seemed a little overdone. He would have done much better wishing me luck and offering to help any way he could. I thanked him for his time, gave him my best smile, and walked right out that open door.

ELEVEN

♦

"Rita, you look terrific."

He said it like he'd forgotten something about the past he was just now remembering and it surprised him. It was strange. I'd done all I could to remind him of what he was missing. I couldn't help myself. I'd stopped in the women's room at a bar across from the subway to put on some more makeup, brush out my hair, and adjust my outfit so it fit just a little bit tighter. It even crossed my mind to give thanks that I'd been more diligent in visiting the "Y" lately, but Frank would never get far enough to see the results.

"Really terrific."

At the same time, I didn't want him to remember too

well. The last thing I needed was Frank trying to get back together with me.

"It's been a long time."

Frank's house was out in Queens. One of those small subdivisions complete with picket fences, flower gardens, and aluminum siding. The next house on either side was no more than three feet away. A Lincoln was parked in front. It could have belonged to someone else, of course. But there was something perfect about imagining Frank behind the wheel of a car like that, so I figured it belonged to him.

"Too long."

I wasn't too thrilled about meeting Frank at his house. It was too personal seeing how he lived now. As if I were involved in his life again. His office was safer. More people. Even if half of them were thieves, dealers, and murderers.

"Things going okay for you now, Rita?"

Only Frank wasn't at the Manhattan South Precinct today. He'd had an attack of gout, too much of the good life it seemed, and was taking it easy at home. Not just today either. He planned to be out the rest of the week. But, hey, that was no problem. Why didn't I just come out to Queens. We could talk about whatever I needed to talk about, I could see the house, and if Carla got home in time, I could even meet his new wife. It sounded just swell.

He'd answered the door in his bathrobe, pajamas, and a cane. A crippled Hugh Hefner, only the pajamas were cotton, not silk. He was still attractive in a newscaster sort of way. Tall. Square-jawed. Hair perfectly in place. Not even a touch of gray. My taste in men from fifteen years ago, freeze-dried and preserved to come back and slap me in the face. He had even mastered the whole sincerity thing. One look into his eyes and you believed anything he said. Unless you knew him.

"Seriously, money, advice, or just a shoulder to cry on. Whatever you need, Rita, it's yours."

I walked inside and it was almost like I'd lived there before. I knew there'd be a couch in the living room, only it was the wrong color and it should have been a little closer to the fireplace. I'd seen these pictures of Frank with famous people before, too. Or others just like them. I'd seen Frank's diplomas and commendations. In a different order, but the same thing. I was tempted to straighten them out but controlled myself.

"I can't tell you how terrific you look, Rita."

"You look good, too, Frank. Someone shot Wilsey."

Frank looked at me, forgetting for a second that he was on the make.

"He's dead. They shot him in my apartment."

"What was he doing in your apartment?"

"I was hoping you could tell me."

"What's it got to do with me?"

He was unnerved. Just a little. Unfortunately, that also made him a little more appealing. I reminded myself to lay off the confrontation stuff. So while Frank poured himself a drink, then limped over to the easy chair and took a seat, I ran through the story for what felt like the hundredth time in the last couple of days. Starting with Wilsey's surprise visit, continuing through his sham story and his book gift, and finishing up with finding him splattered all over my apartment.

"Christ, they assigned that Rantz asshole to your case?"

Frank would understand about that sort of thing. When I looked up, he was nursing his drink. His face was a little paler. A little softer. A little less self-assured.

"How do you like that. Fuckin' Wilsey."

"I'm sorry, Frank."

He shrugged his shoulders. The whole thing hadn't been a part of his life for a number of years and he wasn't the type of guy to let it get to him now. Except maybe for a minute.

"Do they have any leads?"

"They caught someone. His partner. Kid named Sarmiento, but . . ."

"What do you think was going on?"

"I was hoping maybe it had something to do with you. Maybe he'd been in touch. Maybe he wanted something. I don't know."

"No."

"Nothing?"

"Nothing. I cut ties with the guy."

"And you never heard anything about him."

"Stub followed him for a while. Maybe even helped him out here and there. I guess he told me some stories. But I cut ties with the guy and after Stub bought it, nothing. You want a drink?"

He was already halfway to pouring himself another when I got up to join him.

"Wilsey. God, that was such a long time ago." He looked at me as soulfully as he could. "Remember how he'd come over any hour. Catch us messing around half the time. We had some fun, didn't we?"

He'd caught us messing around once as I recalled. I took the drink and retreated as best I could.

"Yes, Frank, we had some fun."

"You seeing anyone these days?"

It was the question I always dreaded. For some reason, whenever I ran into him, he was always just getting married and I was always single, usually just having split up.

"As a matter of fact, there's this professor guy up at Columbia."

It wasn't actually a lie. There was a professor up at

Columbia. I even had plans to see him, more or less.

"That's good, Rita. I hope it works out for you."

He was being sincere again.

"I hope you two are as happy as Carla and I."

Sickeningly so.

"Maybe we could all get together some time. Double-date or something."

"We'll see."

That having been disposed of, we were left with nothing to talk about except Wilsey. Frank hobbled down the stairs to his basement filing cabinets and came back with a thick folder labeled "Weiss." It was a side of Frank I'd forgotten. There was a reason he'd risen in the department. Even without his favor blanket. He was thorough. He was professional. Unfortunately, there wasn't much more to tell than what I'd remembered. Wilsey was an undercover cop who turned. He'd done some good work at first, both for the mob and the cops. Then, for whatever reason, he started doing better work for them.

There was an incident back at the chop shop where Frank thought it all started. Some Bronx street gang was trying to muscle in on the dope trade and got it in their heads that the chop-shop boys were also dealing. They were wrong, of course. Even the mob wouldn't trust real money deals with Fat Stooey Scott.

When they tried to pull a hit on the shop, Fat Stooey did something Wilsey felt saved his life. Frank didn't remember what it was. What was important was that for the first time Wilsey expressed concern for what would happen to Fat Stooey: "Hey, Frank, man, when we take them down, we don't gotta go too hard on Fat Stooey, do we?"

It didn't seem like much to me, but Frank had thought it important enough to write down even then. It got worse with the prostitutes. Interspersed with Frank's reports on

Wilsey's information were personal notes on Wilsey's involvement with several working girls as well as photocopies of several requests Frank had made to get Wilsey out of there. The problem was, Frank had nothing hard to go on. Wilsey wouldn't be the first man on the job to get involved with a pro. In some precincts it was considered an occupational hazard, and Frank's complaining about it would reflect worse on him than it would on Wilsey.

Frank's official reports never mentioned his suspicions of drug use. That kind of thing was for Internal Affairs, and Frank was not the kind to ruin someone's career. But the drugs were all over his personal notes. Suspicions of marijuana. Evidence: smell, yellowed fingertips, attitude change. Suspicions of coke and heroin. Evidence: wild mood swings, nodding off in conversation. He'd crossed the word "tracks" off the page as if that was too dangerous to write down even on a note to himself. Then there was a copy of Frank's request for his own transfer.

"What finally happened to him?" I asked.

Frank had been drinking quietly while I looked through the file.

"You want another?"

I shook my head and watched as Frank refilled his glass, not sure whether the drinking was in Wilsey's honor or something else altogether. I'd heard stories about Frank.

"The guy was useless. They'd set him up for years to be this superwitness. He was going to take down the mob singlehanded. Every time the mayor or council would give us some heat about drugs or crime, someone would pop up about our superagent who would solve the whole thing. Only nobody noticed that our boy was useless. He wasn't only a junkie. He'd been dealing. Trafficking in stolen goods. That whore he was seeing, he had her doing tricks while she was still with him. They would have torn him up on the

stand. Do you know how they found out? The stupid fuck
O.D.'d. Mr. Super Agent. He was useless."

"Did they nail anybody?"

"Yeah. Fat Stooey. He ended up doing three years for the
chop shop."

For some reason we both laughed.

"Do you know what he was working on before he went
down?"

"Not really. Just the usual. Drugs. Extortion. Protection."

There were more details than I'd had before. Maybe even
a lead or two, if you could call nine-year-old information a
lead. Nothing concrete, of course. I don't know if I'd really
expected Frank to be able to hand me the killer's name off
the top of his head, but it seemed the least he could do as
long as I'd had to come see him.

I showed Frank the appointment card. He'd never heard
of Brotell, but he'd check the files at the department to see if
he could find anything. He was more helpful with the drugs.
The brown chunk was opium, something a little more exotic
than most of the garbage that was currently in vogue. The
pills were steroids, about the only drugs I'd be surprised to
find in Wilsey's possession.

"I'll have them checked out if you like, but it looks like
steroids to me."

"Thanks. I think I'll keep them."

"If you want, I can check to see if Wilsey's had a record
recently. Maybe he's been into some shit."

"I already got it from Morris."

Frank just shrugged.

"He must have loved giving it to you."

He was on his fourth drink since I got here, and his words
were coming easy, slurring just the tiniest bit as though it
didn't matter so much what he was saying, just as long as he
had a smile on his face and was saying something that at

least seemed to fit the situation. He had a little sweat on his forehead. His skin seemed puffy. Frank was an alcoholic.

"What happened to Wilsey, Frank. I mean why?"

I don't know why I asked him. Frank didn't like the why question. He never had. But there were two pictures of Wilsey I couldn't get out of my mind. One of a kid at my front door dropping by for dinner. The other of a junkie lying dead on my floor. Frank was the only person I knew who could help me figure out how they fit together.

Frank did his best to think up an answer.

"It wasn't just the drugs. Lots of people do drugs. Wilsey had the self-destruct button. That's all you can say. He had the button. And if it hadn't been drugs, it would have been something else. He was looking to screw up. He'd been planning on it from the day he was born."

It was as much insight as he felt comfortable offering. Then he turned and smiled.

"I meant what I said about you looking terrific."

"Thanks, Frank."

"Why did we ever break up?"

"Because you slept with every bimbo you met and lied whenever I asked about it."

"That'll do it."

He laughed and so did I.

"I'll call you if I find anything about Wilsey. Maybe we could meet some place for a drink."

I nodded and headed for the door, glad the meeting was over. For once, it had stopped raining. As I was walking out the door, a woman came up the block. She was blond. Probably from a bottle. Good figure. And dressing to show it. She wore heels. Nowhere near hooker height, but definitely higher than anything I'd wear. She stood out in the street because she was looking at me. She was looking at me because I was coming out of her house.

Carla probably wasn't a bad person, and it would only do me so much good to lay into Frank's taste in women. But she did look like the kind of woman who didn't approve of the non-dolled-up look. All right, so I was glad I'd put on the makeup and the outfit today. I had no hold on Frank. And I had nothing against his latest wife. Call me a bitch. I gave the new Mrs. Noonan my most enigmatic smile as I strolled past her at the front gate.

TWELVE

♦

I still didn't want to see Malcolm, and seeing Rafe would be even worse. That ruled out going to the office. Home was no good either. It would mean giving up for the day, and I wasn't sure just what I'd accomplished so far. With home and office rejected, I'd usually end up in a bar—a quiet one, where I could look over my notes and decide how to proceed. And have a beer.

Only a beer didn't seem appropriate now. And a hard drink even less so. Not after seeing Frank. Had he always drunk like that? Was it something new? Should I have said something? Was it any of my business? Maybe it was only the Wilsey thing. He wouldn't let his feelings show if he could help it. The drinks would help there. Maybe all the bloat and the thick moves had more to do with the gout. Maybe he wasn't drinking nearly as much as I thought he was. And why should it bother me if he was?

I'd had other friends go down that road before. I'd had friends become junkies. Drunks. Some kicked it. Some didn't.

The ones who didn't usually didn't last too long as friends. I was a big girl. I could write it off. Only Frank was never a friend, even when we'd first started dating.

It was me, of course. I was the one who'd done him in. I smiled even as I thought it. He'd never recovered from our divorce. He'd realized, too late, how rare a person I was, how rare a love I offered, and had spent the rest of his life squandering himself on bimbos and booze. And no matter what anyone said or did, he was destined for the gutter. It was a pretty thought. Only Frank was already drinking when we were together. Probably before that, too. And as much as I'd always felt we could have been good together, there'd always been something missing. Something that would keep things from ever getting close. Maybe what was missing was something stupid that only exists in certain women's magazines. But maybe not. Who knows, maybe not being able to get close to the guy was what attracted me to him in the first place. I hope not. I should have said something.

I was still in the dark about Wilsey, of course. More so than when I'd first started looking. He'd sent away a mob figure, but why would the mob wait so long for revenge? Wilsey'd never left the city. He was even listed in the phone book, for God's sake. And why would they bring him to my apartment?

There were the drugs. They could have been for home use. But where would he get his hands on opium? And what possible use would he have for steroids? That left dealing. But again what did that have to do with me, and what were they looking for in my apartment?

There wasn't much else. A dentist who provided dental care to ex-cops and a package of books that, no matter how significant I wanted them to be, still seemed worthless. A big load of nothing, and nobody paying me anything. If this was what happened now that I was free to control my own time, maybe it was time I found a real job. I wondered where I'd put the paper with the headhunter's number on it.

I was just starting to wonder why I'd felt it necessary to lie to Frank about my seeing somebody and why I was stupid enough to give that lie the quasi reality of Noah Lowell, when it started raining again. I'd been out walking for the last two hours, and for some reason I found myself only a couple of blocks from the office. It was getting late. Maybe there wouldn't be anyone there.

Only there was. There was Rafe, dressed in a waiter's uniform, getting ready to look in on a bachelor party, drumming his fingers on my desk. There was Malcolm, too. Only he didn't look depressed. In fact, he was dressed to the nines. For Malcolm, that is. Royal blue corduroy jacket. Wide yellow tie. He kept looking at his watch as though he was late for another one of those business dinners he needed to have to keep Hannah Lowell's business. And there was Wilsey's super, the short, skinny woman with greasy long hair, a Harley-Davidson T-shirt, and her skeevy kid.

Malcolm and Rafe bolted out the door without a word as soon as I walked in. Bina looked up.

"What's it worth to meet the dead guy's woman, babe?"

THIRTEEN

♦

"That's some swell digs you got there, babe. Hey, Benny, did you see the two desks and that chair that turns and leans and everything? I'm telling you, sugar, you've got a sweet deal."

She'd been talking that way the entire walk back to her place. It was getting dark now. I wasn't sure if she thought she was complimenting me or if she just wanted to let anyone who might be listening in, any potential attacker, know who the rich one was.

"I tell you, though. Your boss, he sure was pissed at you. Hey, I don't care if you're late or what, babe, but he kept looking at his watch and, Benny, did you see how he was getting that little bit of spit in the corners of his mouth?"

Benny was staring off at something somewhere and didn't respond quick enough for Bina's satisfaction. Immediately, a hand whipped out and cuffed the kid across the top of the head. He gave her a look that showed he knew one day he'd be bigger than she was.

"I swear to God, I can't take you no place nice. You ever seen a kid like this? I don't know why God stuck me with him," she said, crossing herself in the process. "You think he's going to fire you, babe?"

I shook my head, trying to limit the conversation to as few words as possible. Sharing language with this woman was far more intimate than I ever wanted to be.

"Hey, well, fuck it, right? He fires you, he fires you. What's it going to help to sweat it?"

That last sentence tailed off. She was losing interest in my situation and had started pulling on her arm hair with some intense concentration.

We finally arrived at the building, and Bina headed straight for her apartment.

"I thought you were going to take me up there."

"You got the money."

We'd agreed on another fifty and I handed it over. Bina pocketed it protectively.

"I said I'd let you know if someone came. Someone came. She's probably still there. But I ain't going up there after dark."

"I'll take her up, Mom."

Bina was quick with the cuff to the head.

" 'I'll take her up, Mom,' " she mimicked. "What am I going to do with the kid? Well, babe, you do what you got to do. If I see something else, I'll give you a call."

Before I knew it, her door was shut and I was standing alone in the hall. If there was a God, I prayed He would make that kid grow bigger than that witch. A lot bigger.

The building was different at night. The cowboy who'd hung around outside was gone. In his place were three young Vietnamese-looking guys with wispy mustaches and slicked-back hair. They were listening to a radio and keeping an eye on who came and left. Unlike earlier in the day when Bina had shown some muscle, she was now frightened. I'd also noticed there were cars parked outside. Nice cars. Not supernice cars that would indicate dealers. Just nice. Cars that definitely did not belong in this neighborhood.

Inside, the building was darker than I remembered, the paint drearier. It was probably a glossy, depressing tan to begin with. The yellow patina from age hadn't done much to improve it. As I climbed the stairs once again, I found myself passing people I wouldn't have expected to see here. People in trendy clothes. People with money. People with glassy eyes. Maybe I should expect the glassy eyes. A strange, Eastern, pulsing music, almost chantlike, with no discernible melody, filtered down the stairs, together with a sweet, sickly smoke.

Wilsey's apartment was a floor below the scene of the action. The same sleazy guy with the gold tooth stood at the top of the stairs like he'd never left. Whatever was going on, it was none of my business. I gave the sleaze a dirty look and knocked on Wilsey's door. There was no answer. I considered how I was going to go about getting my fifty back from Bina. I knocked again.

"Go away."

I knocked again.

"The den's up a flight."

"I'm looking for Wilsey."

This time there was a pause.

"Go away."

It was time to reach for the bankroll again, take a guess as to what kind of bill would get a reaction, and slip it under the door. But I'd been playing that trick a little too often lately and there was no client picking up the expenses for this case. On top of that, I wasn't exactly thrilled about pulling out a wad of cash in front of the guy upstairs, who hadn't taken his eyes off of me.

"I wanted to talk to Wilsey before the police did. If you see him, let him know I'm looking for him."

I slipped my card under the door and waited. After a second the door opened. The woman was thin, bony almost, with long brown frizzy hair and a distracted, wired look in her eyes. She wore tight black jeans that accentuated the anorexic quality of her body and a blousy, flowery almost chiffon top she must have found in some thrift store. Fifteen years ago I'd have pegged her as a speed freak in a second and times had only changed how long it would take to come to the same conclusion.

"You're a detective?"

The standard question. Her voice was overly dramatic, forced, like the way they talk in films about aristocrats now that there are no more aristocrats.

"Yes."

"Like in the movies?"

Each word spat out like the clicks of a telegraph.

"Kind of."

She twirled as dramatically as she could and walked back into the apartment. I followed her inside.

"I'm an actress, you know."

"Really."

"Maybe you've heard of me."

She turned her head to profile and stared up at the ceiling like some old silent film star. I wasn't sure how that was supposed to make me recognize her. Maybe she was famous for looking at ceilings. I shook my head as noncommittally as I could.

"Nell. Nell Imaculata," she insisted, as though if I jogged my memory, I would be sure to remember the fifty or so articles I'd read about her in *People* just the other day in the doctor's office.

I shook my head again. This time she went back to the mattress she'd been lying on, picked up a half-smoked joint, and took a hit.

"Yeah, well, it's been a long time since my last movie. I'm making a comeback, though."

She took another hit, then must have thought about the whole courtesy thing and offered it to me. I passed.

"You live here with Wilsey?"

"Why?"

"No reason."

"I don't have to tell you anything, you know."

"I know."

"I've got my own place. I just come here sometimes when I need to wind down."

As if to punctuate the point, her hand flicked out in the air like a frog's tongue going after a fly.

"How long have you been seeing him?"

"Why?"

"No reason."

"A couple of months, I guess. Or more. Maybe about a year. I don't remember."

This was going to be fun. Just then, a hand pounded on

the door outside. The hand's owner's voice was dull and hollow, but still urgent.

"Hey, open up. Come on. Open."

Without paying any attention to me, Nell leapt from the bed, ran to the door, and screamed back.

"It's upstairs, you fuck. Quit pounding the door. You shit. You asshole. It's up the fucking stairs."

A mumbled "Sorry" passed back from the other side of the door. Nell rolled her eyes and took another hit from the joint.

"Fucking junkies. How are you supposed to live a normal life? Huh? This isn't normal."

I thought about thanking her for the insight but decided against it.

"What's going on upstairs?"

"The den"—as if that answered the question.

"The den?"

"The den. Opium. You know?" Nell rolled her eyes as though I was the most naive human being who ever lived. "They float it. One night here. One night there."

"So the police won't catch them."

"Jesus, you are so smart. No. So they can keep away people they don't want."

It was like the whole disco thing only down a couple of notches. Clubs whose major attraction was that others were kept outside while you were in. Only now it was drugs. Exclusive drugs. Opium. Now you could travel to the most decrepit parts of the city, spend lots of money to become addicted to a drug that only sounded more interesting than heroin, and fortify your social standing at the same time. Who said this wasn't the greatest city in the world?

Enough was enough. If I let this go on any longer, I'd be likely to learn about a cannibal boutique two doors down and find out I didn't get invited to the bestialists' ball at some downtown version of the Waldorf. Some things I was better off not knowing.

"Wilsey's dead."

Nell stopped in her tracks, just staring at me.

"He was shot."

She looked around, nowhere in particular, her eyes finally coming to rest on some ash from her joint that had come loose and landed on the end of her frizzy hair. She picked it off with long nails, the polish of which had mostly chipped off, then shook her hair out and took another hit from the joint. All that in about a second and a half.

"He was shot in my apartment and someone was looking for something and I don't think they found it."

She walked slowly across the apartment until she came back to the bed. Instead of sitting on it, she squatted next to it, wrapping her arms around her knees, and began slowly rocking. Slowly for her, anyway.

"They did it."

"Who did it, Nell?"

"They don't want me to make my comeback. They're afraid. They've got their Jane Fonda and Meryl Streep and Barbra Streisand and Cher and they're afraid of a real actress. They're afraid because they know the public is waiting for me and then those bitches won't be worth shit."

She spat out her words, slowly and deliberately.

"What are you talking about, Nell?"

"There are powerful people out there. People in control."

"And?"

"They knew about Wilsey's book."

"What book?"

"He was writing a book. For me."

"What kind of book, Nell?"

"It was fabulous. He was a cop, you know."

"I know."

"He was writing this great story. It had everything. Action. Money. Fucking. Everything. And it was all true. It was all the truth."

Nell was beginning to perk up, bringing her pace back up to form, aware of the drama of the situation and playing it for all it was worth. Her fingers kept running through her hair, her eyes darting around, her joint rising to her lips.

"For me. He was writing it for me. I was going to play the girlfriend. This whore. And they killed him. They knew he would make me a star and they killed that sweet, sweet boy."

I noticed those were the first words of sentiment she expressed over her deceased lover.

"Are you telling me the book was about his life undercover?"

"Yes. Yes. Yes."

"And he was writing everything he knew before he was fired from the force?"

"He wasn't fired. That's only what they said. They wanted to get rid of him because he knew too much. He was too good. He's been working here undercover to nail the guys who got him."

"Did you ever see the book, Nell?"

She shook her head. "It was too secret. He said if I saw it before they published it, it would put me in danger. They'd have killed me, too."

"Who knew about the book, Nell?"

"He was working with a guy. Big-time. Down at the center."

It took five more questions to figure out the center was Placement Resources, a sort of halfway house for cops leaving the job. Another seven questions and I got a name. Goenther. Was he a writer? An editor? An agent? That was asking too much.

"Anybody else know about the book?"

"Everybody."

Just one more secret for me to be the last to know. I sat there and listened to Nell describe the movie deal she was sure would result from Wilsey's memoirs. I heard her lay into the mob, big business, publishing, the movie industry, and all the trendy shits who had abandoned her when her career began to dissolve years ago. I even finally got to hear about the artist who'd featured her in three of his underground films that changed the history of filmmaking and scared the shit out of Hollywood because they knew that the truth was in New York and so they gave the artist so much money that they cut his balls off and they made him drop her because she was too good only now she was going to come back so they killed Wilsey. And all this time I'd never realized the entirety of history was a conspiracy to suppress a chemically wired has-been, never-was actress.

"You've got to find them."

"I'm going to try."

"You've got to find them and the book."

The sentiment was touching. I couldn't help myself.

"I'm sorry about Wilsey."

"Yeah."

I walked to the door.

"If you hear anything, if you find the book, if someone comes around asking questions, you give me a call. Okay?"

Nell nodded. I left the apartment with a name that could have been nothing more than a hophead's dream and a story that was probably nothing more than a psychotic's paranoia. Still, it was no worse than anything else I had to work with. I noticed that I hadn't heard the door close behind me, and turned to see Nell climbing the stairs one flight up past the omnipresent guard with the one gold tooth.

FOURTEEN

♦

It was late when I left Wilsey's apartment. Late enough to bring some of the nasty people out to the streets. Late enough for me at least to think about taking a cab home. I always figured that would be one of the luxuries of partnership, taking a cab without having to worry about the money. Only now that I'd actually become a partner, all these little bribes were coming out of my own pocket. I skipped the cab and walked to the Chinatown station.

Nell had given me a lot and nothing. Was Wilsey writing a book? Tough to believe from what I saw of the guy just a couple of days ago, but stranger things had happened, and no one said it had to be a good book. Moreover, it would go some way toward explaining why Wilsey showed up at my place when he did. If the book was about the past, and Frank and I were part of that past, at least there was something that might tie him to my apartment.

It might also go a long way to explain Wilsey's present. All right, so he hadn't given me the manuscript. Not the one he was writing, anyway. But maybe he wanted someone to think that he had, someone who was watching him, someone who had a lot more at stake than worrying about Nell's career. Someone who eventually killed him. I didn't feel particularly wonderful about being a decoy, but at this point I was just glad to have something to go on.

There was also another lead to follow: Goenther and Placement Resources. Someone Wilsey had turned to, someone who knew about the supposed book. But there was still a big step to go before making the guy a suspect. Just because he knew about the book didn't mean he was threatened by it. It would require a visit to Goenther's office to figure that out, and it was too late to do it tonight.

By the time I got home, it was almost eleven. Too late for pursuing almost any avenue of the case except feeling bad about how low Wilsey had sunk and wondering what kind of people would spend a warm, dry Wednesday night in an opium den. Normally, that would have been fine. Tonight, though, I needed to do something more. As late as it was, all I could begin to do was check out Nell Imaculata's illustrious film career. And there was only one person I knew who might have the answers.

"Hello, Noah. This is Rita Noonan."

All right, so it was a lame excuse. I just wanted to talk to the guy, clear my head. I wanted to spend a few minutes away from rat-infested, drug-riddled neighborhoods, away from sleazy lowlifes, cowboy half-wits, and deluded stage hounds. I wanted to talk to someone who had nothing to do with old doomed friends or old doomed marriages. At least *my* old doomed marriage. And if he happened to ask me out, that wouldn't be so bad either.

Noah didn't play the "Rita who?" game. He just gave me a warm hello, asked how I'd been and if I'd changed my mind about signing up for film school. Good sign.

"I'm sorry to be calling so late, but I just met this former actress at a party and I was hoping you could tell me something about her. I'd never heard of her. Nell Imaculata."

"What kind of parties do you go to?" he asked, laughing.

"It was kind of one of those friend-of-a-friend things. You know who she is?"

"Sure. She was one of Jiri Bucinski's stars. At least for a

couple of his underground films of the early seventies. She's still alive?"

"Just barely."

I was doing my best to write down the names and information Noah provided. Nell was just an excuse. I hadn't actually expected to get any usable information.

"Was she any good?"

"As an actress? I can't really remember her any more than anyone else in those films. I don't think that was her real name, and maybe she was a rich girl, but they were all awful. That was kind of the point. You never saw any Bucinski films?"

"No."

"You're not missing much. Bucinski's main talent seemed to be conning people to be in his movies. There was a whole scene down there. Tribeca, before it became a neighborhood. A lot of speed and heroin. Art. Guys who were waiting tables and now make several million a year. Junior critics, curators, and gallery owners waiting to make names for themselves. Heavily gay, of course. They were all sleeping with each other, doing whatever they could to make each other happen so they could all get rich."

"Bucinski was part of that?"

"He was kind of at the center of the whole thing. The guy was born rich. He didn't really need anything like the others. You got the feeling watching his films that he was smirking at these people. They were always about these ambitious degenerates who would do anything to claw their way to the top. Imagine a camped-up, low-budget *Sunset Boulevard* and you'll get the idea. I can't believe you've never heard of him."

I was blowing my cover as a film student. What the hell. The alternative would have been researching Nell's past, coming up with a list of these films, then tracking one down and actually sitting through it. It didn't look like I was ever going to do much investigating of Noah Lowell at this point. Finding out about Nell this way seemed far preferable.

"I guess I'd heard the name. I wasn't that into film when he was making movies. How did Nell fit in?"

"As I said, Bucinski's main talent was getting these people to degrade themselves on camera. As though as long as it was all a joke, they should do whatever he wanted them to. And these people weren't just derelicts. Some were artists. Some were junior debutantes. There was even a story going around that one of the girls in his films had four lines, performed oral sex on a transvestite, and he was able to arrange for her to receive college credit for her troubles. I'm not sure exactly what Nell Imaculata's story was, but you could imagine."

"What happened to Bucinski?"

"He finally made a Hollywood film about New York sleaze. The movie bombed. He had a sex-change operation. Then threw himself in front of a subway train."

I put a little X next to Bucinski's name and realized I'd not only run out of questions to ask about Nell Imaculata, I'd completely lost interest in her.

"So."

"So."

"So about that lunch you asked me to," he said.

He remembered. I was sort of hoping that that had been a bad dream, that I couldn't have been that bad an investigator to ask a suspect out to lunch, but there it was.

He continued, "I was thinking maybe we should make it a dinner sort of thing if you don't mind."

There was all the difference in the world between lunch and dinner. Lunch was completely noncommittal. You could have lunch with someone without intentions one way or the other. Married people met other married people for lunch all the time. What the hell. It was only lunch. Dinner was different.

"Dinner would be fine."

"How about tomorrow night?"

"I'd like that."

We arranged to meet at a Village restaurant at nine, then he asked for a work number where he could reach me in case of a change. That was all I'd need, for him to call Malcolm asking for me. With my luck Hannah would be there when he called. It was a scenario I could do without.

"You can leave a message on my home machine. I'll call in."

That all being arranged, I had the sudden urge to dump my problems on the poor guy. To tell him what it felt like to have someone killed in my apartment. And then to have to sleep there. To tell him what it was like to talk to an ex-husband who was falling apart. And to see his new wife for the first time. To dump my problems on him in the hopes that somehow that would purge them. I would have, too, only I didn't think I could explain it all without the detective thing coming into play.

"I'll see you tomorrow."

FIFTEEN

♦

It was one of those waking dreams. Frank was involved. The time was hazy. It was after the divorce, but for some reason he was still in uniform. Aside from ceremonies and funerals, Frank hadn't been in uniform in ten years, but there he was. He hadn't been in my dreams in months, but there he was again.

I'd been having these dreams too often lately. Not with Frank, of course. Usually, the guy or guys were strangers. Usually, it was something that never happpened. The standard pickup at the bar or love-goddess-of-Babylon–type stuff. This time, though, it was more or less my first night with Frank. I didn't mind. That was one of the few nights in our relationship whose reliving would cause me no pain whatsoever. He wasn't in uniform that night. And we'd ended up at my old apartment, not this one like in the dream, but the rest was all the way it happened. Maybe a little glamorized, maybe a little soft-focus, a little romantic, but just the way it happened.

With Frank there had never been that awkward stage. None of that getting to know who likes what where. We'd loved each other like we'd been loving each other for years. Only we still had that first-time thing going for us. That should I be doing this thing. That how well do I know him thing. That danger thing. That he really wants me and God that feels good and I hope it's going to last and please don't stop and Frank, I, sweet Lord, thing.

Damn. It was morning. I was alone. It was still raining. There was no Frank. There was no stranger. Only a buzzer going off in my head. I reached groggily to turn off the alarm, only the buzzing kept going. It was early. Too soon for the alarm. Then what was the buzzing? Maybe the building was burning down.

I thought of returning to sleep, only the damn buzzing made that just about impossible. And my landlord would never spring for anything as sophisticated as a fire alarm. Which meant my doorbell was ringing. Which meant someone had the nerve to be ringing my bell at a quarter to seven in the morning. I staggered as best I could over to the intercom.

"Yeah?"

"Rita, I hope it's not too early." The voice was rough, tired, gravelly, with not much of an inflection in it one way or the other. The kind of voice that could bore you to tears even in that one sentence.

"Max?"

"I have to see you, Rita. I have to," he said, then giggled uncomfortably. "Can I come up?"

I was beginning to come to my senses a little and looked down to see I was wearing only one of Frank's old T-shirts and some underwear. I wouldn't have time to dress if I let him up, and that would drive the poor guy crazy. I hadn't seen Max in months. Not since he'd sworn he'd never speak to me again, which was right after he'd offered to ditch his fiancée in order to marry me and save me from my hazardous line of duty. Max could stand a little torture. I buzzed him in.

I had a few seconds to prepare myself while Max lumbered up the stairs. What the hell, if torture was in order to start the morning, I might as well do it right. I unlocked the door, left it open, and climbed back under the covers.

Max took longer to handle the stairs than I figured. I rubbed my eyes and looked outside. It was raining again. At least Max got soaked for waking me up. A dampness seemed to take up residence inside the air, the sheets, the pillows. Even with the windows open, the apartment was stuffy. It was about to get a whole lot stuffier.

The door swung open. It swung so hard it smashed loudly into the wall. Not that Max intended to make such a dramatic entrance. He just pushed a little too hard. Then he stood in the doorway embarrassed by his awkward gesture. A six-foot-four-inch, two-hundred-eighty-pound, forty-eight-year-old adolescent who'd yet to figure out how to handle the oversized body Nature had handed him. So he slumped his shoulders, let his paunch hang out, and giggled.

"You always leave your door open like this, Rita?"

"I knew you were coming."

"Oh, yeah. Right. 'Cause you can never be too careful. It's a crazy city out there. Believe me, I know from crazy."

He shook his head a little too sincerely. That was to let me know just how concerned he was for my safety. He stood there for a second like he wasn't sure just what to do or say next. He just stood there in his baggy raincoat and crumpled rain hat dripping. I wasn't sure if it was really possible or if there was any way to measure it, but Max somehow seemed to drip more than other people.

"You can hang your coat on the closet door, Max."

"Huh? Oh, yeah. Yeah."

He took the old coat and hat off, revealing a crumpled suit and a head full of flyaway graying hair that looked like he hadn't had time to comb it this morning. It was only at that moment that he realized I was still in bed and though my nether regions were covered by the sheets, I had nothing on under my T-shirt.

"Rita, you're still in bed."

His big face started turning red.

"It's not even seven yet, Max."

"Gee, you should have told me to come back some other time. You are something, kid. Sitting here in your . . . oh, my gosh, if Eileen saw me like this, I tell you I'd be hearing about it for, gosh, who knows how long. Did I tell you I got married?"

"I haven't spoken to you in six months, Max."

"It's been that long? Yeah, well, we did it. Oh, it was a nice little ceremony. You would have liked it. Just family and friends, real tasteful and classy. Like something you'd do the next time, you know, you get married."

It was just what I'd been waiting for. Special bulletins from the department's social pages the moment I woke up. I

had no idea why Max had shown up here. The only thing
was sure of was that he hadn't come here to talk about hi
wedding. I looked over at the awkward giant shifting hi
weight uncomfortably from one foot to the other. If I didn'
turn up the heat a little, I'd be be stuck here all day. I threw
off the covers, walked past him to the kitchen, and turnec
on the Mr. Coffee.

"Coffee, Max?"

"No. No, thanks. Look, maybe I should come back som
other time."

He was staring at my legs as if they threatened him.
wondered whether I'd shaved them recently, but lookin
down right now just wouldn't do.

"Why'd you come at all, Max?"

It was cruel to confront him so directly. At one time he'
been my best contact on the force. He'd been Frank's part
ner and had always harbored something of a fetish for me.
kind of knew I could always turn to Frank if push came t
shove. But this was easier. Less emotional strain. And all
had to do was keep Max's feelings below the boiling point
As much as he seemed to want me, or thought he did, h
was also scared of me. Like the high-school kid sitting in
front of the phone for half an hour working up the nerve t
call the cheerleader. He let me be in control and I did m
best to keep things simple. Only one time I let things go too
far and he proposed. That was the last I'd seen him.

Max giggled one more time, then wiped his forehead ever
though he wasn't sweating.

"It's really raining out there."

The coffee machine started making its semiobscene grunt
ing noises. I stood silently waiting for the pot to fill.

"Look, Rita, you know things haven't been . . . well, you
know how it's been between us. I would've come around
sooner, too. It's just that Eileen doesn't think it's right for a

married father to be hanging around with a single gal like you. Did I tell you she had three kids?"

The coffee was ready. I poured a cup and added some half-and-half from the refrigerator.

"I talked to Frank last night."

I took the cup and walked past him to take a sitting position on the bed.

"He told me about Wilsey. He told me how it happened and everything. How you got involved. How you were working on it."

He suddenly looked around and realized that the murder really did take place right here.

"Where'd they find him?"

I pointed to the floor at his feet. I was sticking with the silent treatment as far as I could. Whether out of respect for the dead or some sort of superstition, Max quickly shifted away from the spot.

"They made an arrest, you know."

"I know."

"But you're still looking into it?"

I nodded. He was shifting around now, more uncomfortably than ever.

"Find anything?"

"Not much. I just started looking. Why?"

Max took a step toward me, then thought I might take it the wrong way and turned to the side into the kitchen. There were only three or four feet for him to pace in. He did his best to make the most of it.

"Rita, all this happened a long time ago. And I'm sure it wouldn't mean much now. But, you know, with this marriage and all, I just don't want anything to go wrong. And Eileen thinks I've got a shot at lieutenant. I keep telling her she's crazy and everything, but you know how cops' wives are. And what the hell, why not let her dream. It's just that I wouldn't want anything to come up that might make me look bad."

He was really uncomfortable now, rubbing his hand over his face, wondering how to approach whatever it was he was trying to approach. It was time to drop the hard line a little and put on my gentle voice.

"What could make you look bad, Max?"

"Look, Rita, this is difficult for me to talk about. Frank doesn't even know about it. But Wilsey. When I heard about it, I don't know, it just drove me crazy. I couldn't sleep. Nothing. You've got to swear you'll keep anything I tell you to yourself. It's just it's all sewed up right now and if you start opening things up, who knows what's going to come up and . . . shit."

He took a deep breath.

"I can't believe I'm telling you this, Rita. Look. When I just made detective, before I hooked up with Frank, I was in a new precinct. Wilsey's precinct. Okay? There were a group of guys on the force, detectives, who were making a little extra on the side, you know. They were on the take. Mostly nickel-and-dime, just a matter of looking the other way when they saw a little gambling. Busting one prostitute instead of another. You know how it works. Rita, I swear I never took a dime. Okay? I was clean. You know me, Rita. Only I was new at the precinct, and you know about the whole Internal Affairs thing. What was I supposed to do? Bust half the detectives on the force? And besides, I never saw anyone actually take any money."

"I never said you did."

"I didn't make any of those busts, Rita. I could have. But I knew all the mob operations under protection and I left them alone. Wilsey knew all about this stuff. He knew who was on the take. He knew what they were making. Hell, he made some of the introductions. When he went down, things just kind of cleaned themselves up. And some of the guys, they've been, you know, taking care of Wilsey ever since. On account of his taking the fall and everything. You've got to believe me, though, this is all old news. And it's got to stay old news. A thing like this could paint the whole precinct as dirty, Rita. I just couldn't handle that. Not now."

"What do you want from me, Max?"

"Drop it, Rita. Please."

I just shrugged. Max was squirming again, only this time it wasn't much fun to watch.

"Do you think it was a cop?" he asked.

"A cop?"

"Who greased him."

"Do you?"

"I don't know. It was so long ago. But if a cop goes down for this, it's going to start a lot of talking."

"Had you seen Wilsey?" I asked.

"No."

"Heard about him?"

"Only here and there. You know. I heard that he'd hit hard times and all, but there've been no new changes. I don't know why anyone would go after him."

I didn't want to worry the guy, but Max would worry whether I told him or not.

"I think Wilsey was writing a book."

"Oh, hell. A book."

"Tell-all. The whole thing."

Max shivered, his whole body shaking for just a second before he brought himself under control.

"You've got to keep me informed, Rita. Let me know what you know. You've got to give me a chance to protect myself and my family."

"Fair enough, Max. Just give me a list of the cops on the take back then."

"You know I can't do that."

I shrugged my shoulders.

"Rita, I can't turn in a cop. There's just no way. I can't. But you find that book, I'll tell you if it's true, okay?"

It wasn't much of a deal. I didn't have the manuscript. Still, it looked like the best I was going to get from the guy. Max was scared. That wasn't all that unusual. The guy was almost always scared, like someone was going to find out he really didn't do all that much around the precinct and he'd sooner or later lose his job. Only this time he looked more scared than usual. Scared enough that he even forgot to take advantage of the opportunity to give me a hug when he left. Considering my state of undress and his usual pattern of behavior, that was something.

"Take care of yourself, Rita. These guys . . . take care."

He put his still-sopping wet coat and hat back on and headed off down the stairs. I locked the door behind him, poured myself a second cup of coffee, then decided I needed a long, hot shower.

SIXTEEN

◆

It was the second time in as many days that I'd heard about cops taking care of Wilsey. Slipping him a couple of bucks on the side. And what Max had said made sense. Rampant corruption in a precinct. One scapegoat takes the fall. Everybody else feels guilty. Or maybe worse. I tried to figure if a guy as wasted as Wilsey would be up to blackmail. I tried to imagine how Frank would feel if he knew

Stub had done something he could have been blackmailed about.

If I'd had any illusions that I could let the Wilsey case ride, Max's visit destroyed them. Now that he knew I was investigating, it wouldn't be long before everyone else did, too. I had to keep going. I'd been working pretty much on what I knew about Wilsey from nine years ago. Now, with the book thing, I had something that tied the past to the present. Only I had to find the book. And that meant trusting the word of a schizzy speed freak. I headed into Manhattan to talk to someone who might know.

There's an accepted practice in the world of charitable organizations of locating the service provided near those needing the service. You don't, for instance, find too many methadone clinics in midtown office buildings. Which is why it seemed odd to find Placement Resources' offices in a steel-and-glass tower on Sixth Avenue. It wasn't that ex-cops found themselves populating the worst sections of the city. But they also seemed to avoid those parts of the city housing what was usually considered to be the city's best. Placement Resources belonged in the residential sections of Queens, Brooklyn, or Staten Island. But here it was, right next to the offices of corporate lawyers and the home bases of international business firms.

And just like its tony location, Placement Resources' offices belied its function. There was none of the hand-me-down furniture and crude artwork of the usual self-help organization. These were digs to compete with those of the heart association and the cancer society. Clean modern design. Soft gray walls. Track lighting. Designer furniture. And everywhere you looked, there were photographs of one man, Mel Goenther, the founder of Placement Resources.

There was Mel Goenther with the mayor. Mel Goenther with the governor. Mel Goenther in his auxiliary policeman's uniform. Mel Goenther with the chief of police and the head of the Policemen's Benevolent Association. Mel Goenther with this Met, that Yankee, and any Knick or Ranger who'd bother to stand next to him. He attended Broadway and restaurant openings alike. This was a man heavily invested in either an evening-wear franchise, Eastman Kodak, or both.

I walked through a waiting room filled with beefy, polyester-clad middle-aged men and women and approached one of the female variety behind the receptionist desk who was wearing a police identification bar over her left breast with the name Betty Kugelmann on it. I handed Ms. Kugelmann my card.

"I'd like to talk to Mr. Goenther."

Kugelmann eyed the card with the usual distrust cops reserved for private investigators.

"Do you have an appointment?" she asked with the nasal half-whine of the native New Yorker.

"I'm investigating the murder of one of your clients. I was hoping he might be able to shed some light on the situation."

It wasn't the standard approach. Normally, I would have come in with some phony credentials and some incredibly wonderful fund-raising idea. I still wasn't as good a liar as Malcolm, though. I opted to live and die with the straight and narrow. Kugelmann gave me a doubtful look.

"Mr. Goenther is a very busy man."

"I'll wait."

I'd been sitting in the waiting room for only a few minutes when this enormously tall, barrel-chested, cocoa-colored black man with close-cropped, thinning hair and a gorgeous suit emerged from the inner offices.

"Ms. Noonan?"

His voice was deep, full, and rich. I got up to shake his hand.

"Ms. Kugelmann just told me about the enormity of your problem and you know I will be happy to help you in any way I can."

Frank used to tell me about cop buffs he encountered here and there. Guys who never actually worked on the job, but for one reason or another knew more about police procedures than most twenty-year veterans. These were the guys who bought all those police-band radios when they were kids, but unlike most kids, they upgraded to more sophisticated models when everyone else was throwing their radio in the closet. He probably had a special room full of nightsticks, handcuffs, and miscellaneous weaponry.

Goenther hadn't spoken two sentences to me and I already knew I'd said the right thing. If I'd asked to see him about a possible fund-raising idea, I'd be sitting out here all day. Involve him in an investigation, and he'd kiss the ground I walked on. I'd take luck over percentages every day.

He ushered me into his large, plush office with a view of the park and more pictures of himself on the walls and poured me a cup of some sort of designer-bean coffee.

"I am so glad you came to see me, Ms. Noonan. You probably want to know a little something about us, hm?"

I nodded and he smiled as if I'd hit upon his favorite subject.

"I made my money in the taxicab industry, beginning with just my own cab and working my way up to a fleet."

He seemed to want some admiration so I gave him some.

"Incredible."

He smiled again.

"During the course of my work I came in contact with a lot of police officers who were working either a second job or were trying to make a second career. Many of them seemed to have a lot of problems, and I felt that something had to be done. We try to fill a need here at Placement Resources, helping those officers who have given so much of themselves to adjust to the rigors of life outside the department. Many of them are older. They've never had jobs outside the force. They hit the age for optional retirement, jump at it, then find themselves unable to cope with the changes. We try to ease that transition."

It was the standard speech, dusted off for every occasion from fund-raising to acceptance speech.

"The officer I'm concerned with never made it to retirement. He was bumped from the force after only a few years."

Goenther drummed his fingers on his desk, trying to give me the impression he was thinking over a serious matter.

"Ms. Noonan, you raise a serious point, one we had to consider deeply prior to forming this organization. What we decided was that we were not a disciplinary board. All police officers deserve at least a chance to make something of themselves after their term of service has ended, for whatever reason."

"Even bad cops?"

"There are no bad cops." Goenther smiled.

"Ms. Kugelmann told me one of our clients passed away. I am so sad. Who was it?"

He was lying. This was the thrill of his week.

"Weiss. William Weiss. His friends called him Wilsey."

For the first time, Goenther looked shaken.

"Wilsey? Wilsey is dead? He said he was in some sort of trouble, but . . ."

"You knew him?"

"He had been coming here for the last seven years. Wilsey was one of our regulars."

"Regulars?"

"We placed him in at least six jobs that I know of since he left the job."

"And?"

"He kept coming back for another one. He was not one of our more successful cases. But he was a character. We had grown affectionate toward him. We would give his case to whoever was new on the staff as a kind of test case. How did he die?"

"Shot."

"Awful. Can I get you another cup?"

He was the soul of graciousness, absolutely at ease in his oversized chair, sitting behind his huge onyx-covered desk. This was a role he was born to play, and I let him play it. The coffee was good.

"You said he was in some sort of trouble?"

"Wilsey was always in some sort of trouble. Naturally, we thought it was financial. He was always involved in one scheme or another. I never thought . . ."

"Can you tell me anything about his most recent visits?"

Goenther called on his intercom for the file.

"Let's see. He had been a bartender. A security guard. He had worked for a moving company. And a custodial service. That was early on. We have no record of any recent employment."

"Does it say anything about a book?"

"You knew about Wilsey's book?"

"You've seen it?"

"Of course not."

"But you just said—"

"Ms. Noonan, every ex-cop swears they're going to write some sort of book. Twenty years of exploits. Twenty years' worth of complaints about the system. Twenty years of stories about the kinds of things you and I just don't see in our daily lives. Twenty years of relatives telling them they should put those stories down in writing. I am surprised you don't know about that, Ms. Noonan."

I let the dig slide past. Goenther was more helpful when he was friendly.

"What about Wilsey?"

"Wilsey, of course, was unique. He only came up with the idea a few months ago. Long since he'd probably forgotten any story he had worth telling. But it doesn't matter. Only one in twenty cops even start the book. One in five hundred finish it. One in five thousand write well enough to do anything with it."

"And Wilsey?"

"I never saw anything."

"He didn't write a book?"

"I never saw it if he did. Still, you could talk to his teacher. We hire a number of writers to help develop our people's writing skills. Even if they never start that book, writing is a valuable skill to have in society."

I was getting a little tired of hearing the guy pat himself on the back, and judging from the kinds of jobs he seemed capable of securing for his clients, I was almost tempted to argue the platitude. I bit my tongue and waited for him to continue.

"Let's see. Wilsey was assigned to Evie. Evie Weber. She's a reporter for *Loisaida This Week*. I don't know if he ever showed up for his classes, though."

I put my coffee cup on Goenther's desk, thanked him for his time, and headed for the door. Just at the last moment I turned around. I was trying to match him in the dramatic gesture department, but without a mirror, I couldn't tell how I was doing.

"Did Wilsey tell you what the book was about?"

Goenther chuckled to himself.

"Something about crime and corruption, I think. The usual stuff."

"Did he say if he mentioned other cops?"

Goenther tightened.

"Why?"

"I'm not sure. There's some indication that there might be some police involvement here."

"Wilsey would not write about other officers."

"Even if he needed money?"

"Never."

"And how would you feel if he had?"

Goenther leaned forward across his desk, staring me down as forcefully as he could.

"Let me tell you, Ms. Noonan. You lay off the cops. Understand? Just lay off the cops."

SEVENTEEN

◆

Judging from the little vein I saw popping in and out on Goenther's forehead, it wouldn't hurt to follow up on Evie Weber as soon as possible. She was the closest lead I had to that book. One call from her boss, and there's no telling how hard it would be to get her to talk. Still, it was almost eleven-fifteen and I hadn't really checked in with Malcolm for a while. He'd be on my case for letting things slide. Moreover, I'd been handing my card out pretty freely. I was hoping Malcolm might have some information.

Malcolm didn't let me down. He had all sorts of information. The rain we'd been getting lately had begun to affect his lungs. He couldn't get a deep breath and he was taking too many pills. The work was backing up. Rafe couldn't get the job done. He could never get the job done. Why did I ever hire him in the first place. And he had an attitude. There'd been words. Something about pay going up and hours coming down. Some kind of threats about leaving. Just when I was gone. Just when he was needed most. Apparently, Rafe was no fool.

On top of that, Hannah Lowell had been calling and complaining how nothing was getting done on her case and what was she paying for anyway. What was going on with that girl at Columbia, Malcolm wanted to know, and when was he going to see some results of my tailing her. He'd already had to take Mrs. Lowell out to dinner two more times just to calm her down and he was getting exhausted and, of course, the cholesterol would kill him. Oh, yes, and Frank had called and told me to meet him at Umberto's in Little Italy for lunch at one.

Of course. Frank called. He'd meet me at Umberto's at one. No thought that I might be busy, that I might already have a lunch date, that I might rather go to some other restaurant, that I might not get the message. Be at Umberto's at one. What with travel time and all, that meant putting off Evie Weber till later, giving Goenther all the time in the world to keep her from talking to me. I wished I did have some plans. I thought about making some up: "Oh, Frank, I'm sorry I missed you. I hope you didn't wait. I figured Malcolm told you I couldn't make it. I was having lunch with . . . a friend."

Only Frank might have heard something about Wilsey, such as how somebody else confessed to the murder, and if I didn't show, I'd probably just hang around wondering what it was. Besides, I hadn't been to Umberto's in a long time, and they did make terrific linguine with white clam sauce.

The only problem was going there with Frank. That's where he'd taken me on our first date, a fact he knew as well as I did. It was also where he took all the women he slept with during our marriage on their first dates. A fact he also knew as well as I did.

Umberto's was low-key, none of the red crushed velvet or fake candlelight you found at many of Little Italy's restaurants. The romance of the place had nothing to do with some prefabricated idea of atmosphere. What it had was incredible seafood, decent prices, and the quality of a special place you could share with the person you discovered it with. No matter how many times that person had discovered it before.

Frank was already sitting at a window table when I got there. If it hadn't been raining, he would've nailed us an outdoor seat. Just as well. I could forgo the romance.

I arrived late to let Frank know he couldn't just mess around with my schedule anytime he wanted, but whatever effect I'd hoped to achieve with the maneuver, I knew I'd blown it when I saw Frank had already gone through half a bottle of wine. I would've felt bad about giving him the opportunity to indulge, only that would've been assuming he hadn't had a pop or two before he even got there. I walked inside and Frank jumped up to give me a hug.

"Rita, I'm glad you got the message. You look terrific."

He was still limping a little from the gout. His voice was thick and his movements were heavy.

"I got the message."

"Hey, you remember this table? We sat here that first time we came here. Remember?"

In actuality, we had sat at one of the outdoor tables. He was remembering one of his other first-time dates. The guy probably had a memory for every table in the restaurant. I could've gotten into the whole thing, but that was a fight from a long time ago, a fight that would have implied feelings Frank would just love me to have.

"I remember."

"I ordered your linguine. I hope you don't mind."

"That was nice of you, Frank."

"And this wine."

He poured some into each of our glasses, finishing off the bottle in the process. Almost automatically, he signaled to the waiter to bring a second bottle. Frank didn't give me a chance to start in on him.

"Bobby Sarmiento just walked."

Frank was smiling. Like he'd completely forgotten the murdered man was once his best friend. And the only thing that mattered was that he'd done something that might cause me to owe him a favor. He loved nothing better than helping a woman out. Every woman's big brother, a real sweetheart.

"He murdered an ex-cop," he said.

"The kid says he's innocent."

"What a surprise."

The linguine arrived. So did the wine. Frank poured himself another glass and continued.

"They never charged him with the murder. Just a breaking-and-entering case they had some proof on from a while back. They're stalling till they can find something that will tie him to our old apartment."

"What if he runs?"

Frank shrugged.

"Do you want to see him?"

"You have his address?"

"I'll do you one better. I'll take you to him. He works only about ten blocks from here. I called and told him we'd be coming."

If Frank's eyes were dull when I got here, they were

sparkling now. The whole thing was a setup. A plan to get back into my life using Sarmiento as the wedge. Whether I got something out of this or not.

"I'll take the address."

"Don't be silly. You never know about these guys. You'll be glad to have me along. Come on. We'll eat a little lunch, drink a little wine, then go check out the scumbag. It'll be fun. We've never worked a case together."

Having decided how great it would be to work together, Frank wanted to know more about the case. He didn't know anything about the book, of course. It didn't sound like Wilsey was in much shape to write something like that, but of course he could have convinced someone to ghost it for him if they thought he really had a story to tell.

"Would he have a story, Frank?"

"Sure, I guess. The mob stuff. The undercover life. It depends what kind of stuff you like to read, but he could have a story."

"What about cops?"

"Cops?"

"Were there any dirty cops in the precinct back then?"

"Hey, I don't know about that stuff."

Frank tried to come across as free and easy, but on the subject of corruption he gave no ground. Anytime he'd come to a new precinct, he'd lay out his position. He wouldn't go looking for anything, but what he found out, he'd report. If a cop was dirty, it was his responsibility to keep it small enough that Frank would never find out. No one talked to Frank about things like that. It was simple blissful ignorance.

So that was that. We had nothing left to discuss on the case. I still had a few more bites of linguine, so Frank took the opportunity to order one last bottle of wine. Was this his normal consumption? Was he just saving up because he wouldn't be able to grab another drink before dinner?

I couldn't help thinking of Wilsey. How Frank saw him when his slide began. How he'd never said anything—the whole professional courtesy thing. He'd just watched Wilsey blow his whole life away, a little piece at a time. And now I was about to do the same thing with Frank.

Maybe Frank anticipated what I was thinking. He was a good cop. No reason to think he couldn't. Whatever, he cut me off before I could say anything.

"You know, Carla saw you leaving the other day. You wouldn't believe what she thought."

I could hear him explaining things to his wife. I'd heard the same explanations myself only a few years ago. It didn't make much difference that this time the explanation was true. There would be all those occasions she didn't find out about that would more than balance that account.

"It's funny. She said she was going to leave me. She's always giving me a hard time about this and that. Hell, she's always giving me a hard time."

Frank took a deep sip from his glass. Somehow the complaining made the drinking acceptable. At least I wouldn't say anything under the circumstances. He was staring into the glass, the classic drinker's pose.

Suddenly, he smiled. It was the same Frank smile he was always able to whip out at a moment's notice, the one that got him out of more trouble than it should have, the one that made the marriage last much longer than it should have.

"You know," he said, "I guess I just don't have much luck with women."

EIGHTEEN

♦

We walked for a while after leaving Umberto's. A little south, a little east. Toward a kind of no-man's-land that flirted with Chinatown and the South Street Seaport. One good thing about having Frank with me was not having to pay attention to the neighborhood. With the whole crack thing the way it was and with the neighborhoods I'd been traveling in lately, I didn't mind knowing Frank never traveled anywhere without a gun and would make it a matter of pride to handle anything that came up. That left me free to wonder how I was going to get rid of the guy.

Sarmiento worked at a parking garage that didn't seem to serve any one particular location. Too far from Chinatown or City Hall or Wall Street, the lot nevertheless seemed to be thriving, with a line of cars pulling in even while we approached. A tall Indian with a gut and a black "Guns n' Roses Was Here" T-shirt sat in the payout booth listening to loud heavy-metal music.

Frank flashed his badge.

"Bobby Sarmiento?"

The Indian didn't even move.

"Fourth floor."

The English was accented and completely dispassionate. The guy had no feelings about setting Sarmiento up.

"Thanks, buddy."

Frank gave the guy a wink, and we entered the dark building. This was a tall, narrow garage; with end walls no more than thirty-five feet across. Cars were jammed in wherever they could fit. There must have been a stairway somewhere, but Frank preferred to walk up the crisscrossing ramps. The sounds of squealing tires echoed here and there throughout the place. The lights were dim. Whenever a car did pass by, heading one way or the other, they needed lights to see where to go. Once again Frank was the leader.

As we got near the fourth floor, we could hear voices in addition to the car noises we'd been hearing. Sitting around an old picnic table that looked like it had been picked out of a suburban junk heap were three cardplayers, all wearing dirty uniforms, none of which matched. Their conversation was mostly limited to muttering, since, as we got closer, it became apparent that none of them spoke the same language. The only words I understood were the lyrics to the music coming over a car radio they had running.

Frank walked right up to this wiry Hispanic-looking guy with bad teeth and a crew cut and dropped his badge on the table.

"Hey, Bobby, glad to see me? Why don't you tell your friends here that the game's over."

Bobby rolled his eyes and the other two shuffled away resignedly.

"How've you been doing, Bobby? Not thinking of skipping bail, are you?"

Frank was needling the guy. Whether it was his usual style of operation or he was just showing off for me, I wouldn't know.

"I've been good. What you want?"

Frank walked around the nearby cars, touching one, leaning against another.

"You make good money here, Bobby? Four, five dollars an hour? That pay for your habit?"

"I've been good."

"How much you get for switching batteries? What about a spare tire? You got the nerve to boost a radio once in a while?"

Frank was definitely showing off. Even Sarmiento knew it. For the first time, he looked up and noticed me.

"Who's the bitch?"

It was one of those quaint figures of speech that could really help you warm up to a guy.

"My ex-wife. You got a problem with that?"

No private investigator. No partner. Just "My ex-wife." I couldn't blame Sarmiento for laughing.

"Hey, baby, you want to see a good time, you give me a call."

It was time for Frank to top his tough-guy act by giving him a backhand to the guy's jaw, but there was a limit to Frank's showing off. Frank looked at me, looking for I'm not sure what. I just smiled. This was his show for now. Let him get on with it.

"They're going to nail your ass for the Wilsey murder, Bobby."

"I didn't kill nobody."

"You want to talk about it?"

Sarmiento picked up the cards and began shuffling absentmindedly. He'd lost some of his attitude with the murder talk. It looked like he was trying to get it back.

"Shit happens, man," he shrugged off.

"What do you know about it?"

"Nothing."

He would have said nothing no matter what his involvement in the case.

"Nothing?"

"Hey, man, give me a break. I don't know everything the dude was into. If someone offed him, hey, I guess I'm just lucky I wasn't in on the deal. Who knows? Maybe I just wasn't around. Maybe they're still looking for me. Maybe I need some protection. How about that, chief, you going to get me some protection?"

He hadn't been ruffled at all. He just kept sitting at the table, shuffling the cards automatically.

"Do you need protection, Bobby?"

"You tell me."

"What do you know, Bobby?"

"I don't know shit."

For all his showing off, Frank was screwing up. It was time for me to take a turn.

"What do you know about a guy named Dr. Brotell?"

I wasn't sure who gave me the dirtier look, Frank or Sarmiento.

"I'm a private investigator. Wilsey was killed in my apartment. Your wife asked me to help you. If you want to go down for this thing, I could give a shit. Now, what do you know about Brotell?"

Bobby looked at me as if he wasn't sure whether to bare his soul or break out laughing. Then he looked at Frank.

"Take a walk, Frank," I said.

Frank's plan to save my butt was unraveling before his eyes. But Sarmiento would never talk to a cop. Even to save his own life. Frank turned away stone-faced.

"I'll meet you outside."

Sarmiento waited till Frank was out of earshot.

"You not a cop, lady?"

I shook my head and handed him my card.

"What they got on me?"

"How should I know? I'm not a cop. You knew the guy. You did crimes together. He used to be a cop. They can't just drop it. Figure it out."

Sarmiento was beginning to get nervous. The kinds of crimes he usually did put him back out on the streets in at most a couple of months. Murder was something else. And if the guy was an ex-cop, there'd be no plea-bargaining either. Bobby Sarmiento was probably innocent, of course. But there's something about innocence, about going up for a crime you didn't do, that seems to scare the hell out of a guy who sits around laughing about all the times he's beaten a sentence for something he did.

"I didn't do it."

"Who did?"

"I don't know."

"Tell me about Brotell."

"The dentist? What you want to know?"

"Is he selling steroids?"

The question was a little too direct for a guy like Bobby, even if it wasn't coming from a cop. He shuffled the cards for a while. And when he finally started to talk, his eyes looked off sideways into the dark part of the garage.

"We used to hustle for the guy a little. Hang out in gyms, high schools, you know."

"Wilsey, too?"

"Sure."

"Wilsey ever take from the guy? Pocket anything?"

Sarmiento just shrugged.

"Would Brotell kill him?"

"That guy was a pussy. He still lives with his mama."

I nodded. Brotell had struck me as something of a dabbler as well. Started out taking the drugs himself, then realized how much money he could save if he started selling. Too greedy to get out of it, too scared to go big-time. Murder seemed just a bit over his head.

"What about blackmail, Bobby?"

"Blackmail? Who's he going to blackmail?"

"Cops?"

The shuffling stopped for a second, then resumed.

"Hey, lady, I don't know nothing about cops."

"Did Wilsey?"

"I don't know."

"Did he ever talk to you about a book he was writing?"

"No."

"Did you kill him, Bobby?"

"No."

The noes had begun coming with too much regularity for my taste. Sarmiento was done for the day. All that was left for me to do was scare him enough to make him consider the possibility of another session.

"Be careful, Bobby. If you did the hit, the cops will be watching for you to make a mistake. If you didn't, things could be even worse."

Sarmiento smiled as disarmingly as he could.

"Don't worry, lady. I'll be good."

"Let me know if you hear anything."

"Don't worry, lady, you will definitely hear from me."

The feeling of reassurance that provided me was overwhelming. As I turned to leave, he couldn't resist adding a little something.

"No wonder you left him, lady. He really don't have no class."

I walked away to the sound of his laughter. Frank was waiting for me at the entrance to the garage, just like he said he'd be. He seemed off somewhere on his own, as if he was really tired, and just wasn't paying much attention to where he was or what he was doing.

"Frank . . ."

"Huh? Oh, what? Hey, sorry I didn't get more out of the guy. What did he say?"

"I'm going to handle the rest of this thing on my own."

"Why? I thought we were getting someplace."

"No reason. I just work better on my own."

It was like he was expecting all sorts of gratitude. Like he'd expected to come in, spend half an hour on the case, wrap the whole thing up all so that I'd cozy up to him with the big-hero thing. When it wasn't that easy and I wasn't that grateful, he wasn't sure exactly what to do. He turned to his old standby.

"Come on. Let's find a bar and we'll talk about it."

"I'm not going to a bar with you, Frank."

"What's that supposed to mean?"

"Kill yourself if you want to. I'm not going to help."

"Wait a minute. You think I've got a drinking problem or something?"

"In a word?"

It was the most focused I'd seen Frank in years. He wasn't trying to put one over. He wasn't trying to make an impression. He wasn't trying to get laid.

"Who the fuck do you think you are, Rita? Huh? My mother? My wife? Is that it, Rita? You think you're my wife? You've got no right. No right."

Frank's outbursts had raised some eyebrows from the passersby. He now had to walk off followed by their stares. I watched him go, longing for the good feeling I was supposed to get from doing the right thing.

NINETEEN

♦

I went straight to a pay phone. Evie Weber had already left for the day. I could have tried to worm her home phone or address out of the *Loisaida This Week* receptionist or maybe tried to call all the E. Webers in the phone book or break out the book of professional associations and hope Ms. Weber was a member in good standing of whatever association press people were supposed to be members of. The temptation was to spend all sorts of time tracking her down now, but Goenther had already had plenty of opportunity to call if he'd had a mind to. Talking to her tomorrow would do just as well, and would save me most of an afternoon's work.

Bobby Sarmiento had done his best to write off Dr. Brotell as a suspect and I was inclined to agree. The guy was working too hard at it to really be dangerous. Only hunches sometimes go wrong and not checking them out could become a dangerous habit. So with nothing else to do and the rain having pretty much let up, I positioned myself across from Brotell's brownstone. There was little doubt now he was pushing steroids, and Sarmiento even let me know kids were involved. The only thing I wanted to know was, did he kill Wilsey? Until I figured out a way to check that out, watching him seemed as good an idea as any.

I set up shop across the street in a stairwell down to a basement apartment. I had a clear view of Brotell's front door, but, being below sidewalk level, I didn't give him much of a view of me. That was about all I could say for the perch. It wouldn't have been much protection if the rain had resumed. There was an overhang on the building's roof that would've dumped most of the overflow on my head. Even worse, it was a residential building, which meant the possibility of suspicious neighbors and unwelcome visits from the uniformed members of the force.

Still, I'd anticipated most of those problems. What I hadn't anticipated was the pair of Yorkshires belonging to the occupant of the basement apartment, doing their best to call me to the attention of their owner or a neighbor. If anyone was home, though, they must have been used to the noise and ignored it. The two little creatures, one with a bow in its hair, yipped the entire hour and a half it took for Brotell to appear.

He shut the door to the building and headed over to Second Avenue accompanied by a short, squat woman with white hair dressed as stylishly as short, squat women with white hair tend to dress. I said a quick good-bye to the yipping dogs and headed after them. Brotell and his mother picked up a newspaper at the corner. So far, they'd broken no laws. That was the frustrating part of the job.

A half hour later I'd followed them to their launderer and watched Mrs. Brotell argue over something like starch in her son's athletic shirt. I'd documented his buying a bottle of Evian and several bottles of vitamins from the health-food store two blocks farther away. Then, after dropping his mother off at a self-consciously quaint tearoom populated mostly by other similarly dressed women, I'd even seen him check out a woman jogger as she ran by. None of his actions was even remotely suspicious. The most damning thing he'd done was make a call from a pay phone. There were all sorts of things to read into the fact that he left his office to make a call on a noisy city street, but without a bug of some sort, my suspicions would remain just that. I made a note of the phone he used and followed behind him.

Brotell's next stop was more promising. Langdon's Gym was not one among the wave of health spas that had surfaced in the last couple of years. There were no hanging plants, no little restaurant serving fruity concoctions with even fruitier names. It was an older brick building and the club members were interested only in boxing and weight training. This was a gym that had been around for the last fifty years and would probably still be there long after its newer cousins were gone.

If Brotell had belonged to a different type of club, I might have been able to fake my way in. Ask for a free trial to see if I wanted to join and work my way through the weight machines while he did his thing, keeping an eye on him all the time. I was in reasonably decent shape now. I went to the "Y" a couple of times a week and ran once in a while if I felt some particular need to punish myself. But even though I felt pretty good and, when the lighting was right, could see some muscle definition in my arms, I'd never pass for a bodybuilder. Especially not here.

Powerfully built men and women, all of them taller than Brotell, walked past me into the building. Outside, a group of muscle boys hung around like kids after school. There wasn't much point in going farther. Brotell was selling, but there wasn't much chance he'd be handling the stuff himself. Not here anyway. Not at his own gym. Not unless he thought it might get him into the pants of some muscle queen. All that would come of hanging around now would be to hassle him. Still, all work and no play . . .

I psyched myself up to do my best jock walk and headed over to the gang lounging outside the gym. There was no way my body would pass inside, but out here, under a coat, wearing pants, I at least had a chance.

"Hey, got a minute?"

I'd picked out the only scrawny guy in the group, a pale blond kid with some hair here and there above his lip who looked like he'd stepped out of the movie *Deliverance*, figuring he looked like he belonged here just about as much as Wilsey would have.

"Yeah?"

I took the kid aside and ran through the entire rap of how I'd been lifting for a year now and was looking for a way to bulk up. I did my best to be convincing, but it didn't much matter. What I wanted was to find out what Brotell would do if he thought I was threatening him.

"Well, how am I supposed to know where to find that stuff?"

He was playing it innocent, but he hadn't walked away. My card being inappropriate for the occasion, I tore a piece of paper from my little notebook and wrote my first name and phone number on it.

"Do you know a guy named Brotell?"

The kid shook his head.

"Little guy. Pretty ripped. A friend said he could help me out. Said he works out here."

Once again the kid shook his head.

"Give me a call if you hear something."

I hadn't planned to stick my neck out like this when I'd set out to follow Brotell. Only now that I'd done it, there was no reason to hold back. The odds that this kid would ever call were slim. They weren't all that much better that he'd even get the message back to Brotell. But now that I'd already laid myself out as bait, there was no reason to hold back from the more direct approach.

I knew Brotell was inside the gym, and I had no reason to talk to him now. I stopped at a pay phone and called the answering service that was covering for him. I told them my

name was Rita, that I was looking to bulk up, and that I'd
heard his name around. I wanted to make a purchase. I'd be
in touch.

I wanted to let on enough of my suspicions to make
Brotell nervous about my sharing them with his answering
service. Whatever his involvement, he'd want to quiet me up
as quickly as possible. I gave my first name so he'd have a
pretty good idea just who it was he'd want to hush up. It
was a great feeling. Something akin to what the worm feels
when the hook goes through him.

TWENTY

♦

There was enough time to get home, change, and still get
back in time for dinner with Noah. Only that would have
been admitting this was a date. Something to dress for.
Going straight from work kept things casual. Almost. Of
course, that meant hanging around in the city for an hour
first.

I got to the office a little after seven-thirty. Malcolm was
still there. Alone at his desk, he grabbed for some papers
when he heard me come in. A jacket I'd never seen before
was hanging on the coatrack. He was still wearing his tie, a
minor miracle this late in the day. And his top button was
still buttoned. The odor of after-shave permeated the room.

"What are you doing here?"

"I was working on the Wilsey thing."

Malcolm snorted.

"Well, you should call before you come."

It wasn't worth arguing. He looked down at his watch nervously.

"I'm meeting someone. A client."

I nodded. We sat across from each other, not saying anything.

"Did you follow that girl at Columbia yet?" he asked.

I shook my head.

"I told you she was a dead end," I said.

"And I told you to follow her. I don't pay you to think."

"You don't pay me at all. The business does. I'm a partner. Remember?"

"I'm going to forget the biggest mistake of my life? Forty years I'm in this business. In one you're going to kill it on me."

It was the kind of thing he might have said in his usual obnoxious style of kidding around, but there was no humor in his voice and his fleshy face had turned nearly purple. We sat there quietly again for a moment and I watched while Malcolm grabbed for his pills. Maybe it was time to find out how much my services would bring on the open market.

"So, you getting anywhere?" he asked.

It came out of nowhere and was as close to an apology as I was likely to get. I did my best to brief Malcolm in as little time as possible, telling him about bad books, bad cops, bad actresses, bad dentists, and a bad guy who'd just been let out of jail.

"You're still fishing."

I agreed. Malcolm checked his watch.

"What are your instincts?" he asked.

The old guy still worked in the old style. He'd picked up a computer a couple of years back but didn't know how to use it, even for doing the books. These days the big-money agencies used them for just about everything. The kind of work I was doing would be handed to the entry-level types. Instincts weren't much in demand. Malcolm had just about nothing else, so he elevated them to a near-mystical level.

"I'm going to see Wilsey's writing teacher tomorrow."

"Good."

That was just about the time the door opened and Hannah Lowell walked in. If I'd thought Hannah was decked out the first time I'd seen her, I hadn't seen anything yet. There was nothing so much that was different; there was just more. Thicker makeup, higher heels, more cleavage. It was look-at-me, want-me time. No matter how Malcolm wanted to disguise it, this was no business dinner.

Hannah took one glance at me and turned to Malcolm.

"Is she still working here?"

I guess that meant I didn't have to ask if she'd heard about Wilsey being murdered in my apartment. To my surprise, Malcolm jumped in to defend me. Something about the murder not being my fault, how I was never even brought to the precinct, how I was helping the police with the investigation, and how having an old friend murdered in your apartment could happen to anyone. That last part didn't even convince me.

"I want her off my case."

Even if it would relieve one complication from my life, I didn't relish her tone. And it didn't make me feel much better to listen to Malcolm's protests. They wouldn't work and only made me feel more pathetic. Malcolm just assumed someone would have to be talked into wanting my services.

"She hasn't even done anything. You said I'd have some results in a day or so. I've got nothing. I want her off my case, Malcolm."

It was the first time I'd heard her use his first name, but this was no little intimacy. She was giving him an order and

Malcolm would take it. He shifted his weight, rocked forward in his chair, and stood up.

"Come by the office in the morning and we'll talk," he said to me.

He said it in his most ominous voice, then turned and followed his favorite client out the door. One more trouble I didn't need. It was a shame Hannah was so insistent about removing me from the case. I was about to find out all about her husband.

TWENTY-ONE

◆

I was still sitting at my desk at a quarter to nine. Village Hunan was a good half-hour walk from here. That meant I'd be late unless I took a cab, which right now was beyond my budget. There was no reason to keep Lowell waiting, and I certainly had no interest in making an entrance. Ambivalence was more like it. Did I really want to be going out with this guy tonight?

The problem wasn't that his wife was a client. I'd already screwed that up pretty well. The problem was that he still had a wife. I'd been single most of my life. My time with Frank only lasted a little more than five years. But before and after Frank, I'd never gone out with a married man. It wasn't a big deal. Not like I'd sat down one day and made some sort of vow to uphold the solidarity of sisterhood. Even as a former cheated-upon spouse, I never blamed the women Frank had it off with. Much. I wasn't wild about

them, but they had nothing to do with what was wron
with our marriage.

But even if I had no fixed feelings on the subject, tha
didn't mean I should go jumping in bed with the fir
married guy to come along. Not, of course, that Noah ha
asked me to jump into bed with him, but that was als
beside the point. The point was that there was something t
think about. And for better or worse, Noah Lowell was sti
married. And right now, when I was supposed to set off fc
dinner with her husband, the wife's face kept going throug
my mind. That didn't mean I wouldn't go. It just meant he
face was in my mind a lot more than I cared for it to be.

It was getting later. The ambivalence was giving me a
out. Leaving now wouldn't get me to the restaurant ti
almost nine-thirty. Maybe he'd have left. Maybe he'd hav
made all the decisions for me. The decision about going ou
with married men. The decision about making a mess of m
career. Not to mention the decision about getting involve
with anyone at all. It had been several months since my la
relationship, and I'd blown that one completely. It wouldn
kill me if either he'd already left or was totally pissed o
when I got there. With that spirit of joyous optimism,
locked up the office and headed across town.

Village Hunan was a chain of relatively upscale Chines
restaurants. No red. No gold. No dragons. No lanterns. Ju
an occasional tasteful landscape on the wall. The owne
were trying to position themselves as a restaurant more tha
an experience. It was a good choice. A steakhouse woul
have marked Noah as stodgy; vegetarian, as self-righteou
And I never ate Thai on the first date. Chinese was sa
without being too safe.

The only thing missing at Village Hunan when I got the
was Noah Lowell. And for some reason I knew he hadn
come and gone. I hadn't expected him not to show up, and

1adn't expected to feel disappointed. To feel like I'd been
stood up. Like our evening together meant more to me than
t had to him. Like I was alone, humiliated. I didn't measure
up. I didn't matter.

I should have called it a night and gone home. Admit I'd
been blown off and forget about it. Only I was still hungry,
and I'd worked up a taste for Hunan. And who knows,
maybe Noah would still show up. Suddenly, it seemed important to see him.

I had finished my fried dumplings and was halfway through
the orange-flavored chicken when Noah Lowell finally walked
through the door at ten-fifteen. It would have been nice if
he'd run over to my table, removed my shoes, and began
furiously kissing my feet. He didn't. He even seemed to be
considering walking right back out the door. But he didn't
do that either. Instead, he walked over to my table.

"I almost didn't come," he said with a sad half smile.

No sorry. No begging forgiveness. Nothing. Somehow
that made the whole deal a little easier.

"I was a half hour late myself."

"Even after I decided to come, I was walking around
outside for a while wondering if I should."

"It's only a dinner, Noah." For some reason I was doing
my best to bring him around. "Have a seat."

Noah caught my smile and returned it. Without much
more thought, he pulled out the chair and lowered his tall
thin frame into it.

"I got a call from my wife today. Great way to start the
conversation, right?"

"Are you looking for a shoulder?"

"Not really. It's just strange. She called to tell me she was
having an affair and wanted to let me know. Some older
guy. She was going out to dinner with him tonight."

I stifled a cough and he shook his head in something that

looked like amusement, then saw the waiter passing by and ordered a beer and a bowl of cold sesame noodles.

"Did that bother you?" I asked.

He thought about it for a good several seconds. Of course he only had the image of his wife to work with. It was my good fortune also to be able to picture the old fat man she'd be sitting across from.

"No." Then he laughed. "I mean I guess I'd prefer not to know about such things. I'd prefer not to know he was wealthy. I'd prefer not to know he could take her out to nicer restaurants than I ever could. I'd prefer not to know he was buying her jewelry I probably wouldn't even like but could never afford anyway. But in a way it relieves some of the pressure. I don't have to worry about her crying her eyes out at home, do I?"

Indeed he didn't. And suddenly Malcolm's words about the business doing badly echoed so loudly in my head I was surprised Noah didn't hear. Where exactly did he get the money to treat her like Noah couldn't. The whole topic was as sure a way to ruin what was turning into a pleasant evening as any I could think of.

"I'm glad you decided to come in."

He smiled back, but only for a moment.

"Yes, well, that was only half of it."

The conversation was beginning to take an ominous turn.

"You see, I was working this afternoon on a paper on Bresson's *Un Condamné à mort s'est échappé* and I thought of you. Do you like Bresson?"

"Bresson?"

"How about Ozu? Or Renoir? Or Hawks? Or Ford?"

"John Ford, right?"

My dad always liked Westerns.

"And I couldn't tell what camp of theorists you came

down in. Bazin? Lacan? Metz? How do you feel about deconstruction?"

I could have tried to bullshit the guy with some vague talk about film and culture and maybe my favorite movies, and if I'd known even a little bit about what I was talking about, the temptation to do that might have been irresistible. As it was, I took a sip of my beer and waited for him to go on.

"My point is . . . who are you? I've been thinking about it all day. You come into my class, listen to one lecture, then ask me out. This doesn't happen every day."

He was smiling now. Still serious, but smiling.

"Don't underestimate yourself."

"You're not a prospective student at all, right? I mean, you have no interest in film studies. Don't worry, I won't hold that against you."

What I needed was a good lie. I mean, I couldn't tell him I was spying on him for his wife. Only nothing came to mind, no simple explanation of what I was doing in his classroom. Noah let me sweat for a minute before jumping in.

"Don't get me wrong. I'm flattered and everything. I'm glad you asked me. I just don't believe you sat through a film-theory lecture because you liked me."

"I'm looking into journalism."

"Film reviews?"

"Investigative reporting."

It was a lie, but at least I could pretend I knew something about investigating.

"And you wanted to investigate the scourge of corruption in the Columbia Film Department?"

"Promise you won't get mad?"

"Okay."

"I came in to get out of the rain."

Noah looked at me for a second.

"You're still lying."

I was, but this was the best I could do. If I had to try again, I'd probably come up with something about getting chased into his class by a pack of wild dogs or sitting in on every class in the university on a bet. I figured I'd better sit quietly and wait for him to come up with an idea.

"You came in because you thought I was cute."

So the dinner progressed. We got along like I'd been afraid we would. He didn't swear undying love or pop a ring out of a box. He didn't even offer to pay for the meal. We just had a few beers and talked and ate. And whatever eventually happened tonight, I knew we'd be seeing more of each other.

That still left me with what was going to happen tonight. Was I ready for a relationship right now? And what would be appropriate behavior? A kiss? More? What would he want? What did I want? Where would we end up going after dinner?

We were finishing our last beers. Noah looked up and smiled.

"I'm still not sure I trust you."

"You're breaking my heart."

"I'm sure. Look. There's a Bresson festival at Cinema Village next week. Want to go?"

And that was it. No invitation back to his place. No offer to take me home. He just split the check, gave me a quick kiss, and headed off into the night. I was used to taking subways home alone. Most guys who found out I was a private investigator figured I could take care of myself. Only Noah didn't know I was a detective. If he figured I could take care of myself, it was for some other reason.

Either that, or he wanted to let me know that he still wasn't ready to take responsibility for me. If this was going to happen, I was going to have to pursue it. Hannah was wrong about her husband. Noah wasn't out looking for anything. I guess I was. At least Hannah was right about something.

I was putting the key in the front door when I felt a hand on the back of my shoulder.

"Where you been, Noonan? I've been waiting a long time."

TWENTY-TWO

◆

Jesus Rantz was so close I could smell the onions from his last chili dog. There was a damp chill in the air, but I could feel the heat from his body, smell the sweat on him. His hand stayed clamped on my shoulder; in no way violent, just there.

I looked at his eyes. The look of a dog getting ready to attack. I tried to remember that Frank had a look like that. One he could turn on and off. One he used to turn up the heat whenever he needed it. A simple tactic, nothing more or less, I tried to tell myself. Only it didn't help. Maybe it was the pockmarked skin, the deep-set sleepy eyes, or the long skeevy fingers that still clutched my shoulder. The son of a bitch scared the hell out of me.

"I'm surprised at you, Noonan. Going out with a stiff like that."

"Get your hand off me, Rantz."

He'd take his hands away when he was good and ready, but it wouldn't hurt to stand up to him early. My fingers curled around my keys as I tried to decide which eye of his to drive them into if I had the opportunity. Rantz pushed his weight against me, leaning into the front door of the building.

"The guy shows up late and didn't even pick up the tab. Bad show, Rita. You must be getting a little desperate these days. And to top it off, you didn't even give the poor guy a little taste. I'm surprised, Rita. Word around the precinct always was that you were on the easy side. Is that true, Rita? Are you easy?"

He was going to keep talking, which meant I was going to keep listening. At least until he got around to telling me what he was doing here. For some reason he got a kick out of letting me know he'd been following me all night. Probably figured it would give me the creeps. He'd figured pretty well.

"And the guy wasn't even on the job, Rita. What would Frank say? What are we going to talk about down at the station if you've stopped doing cops? Baby, you've got to come back to the fold."

"With you, Rantz?"

"Hey, maybe if I checked you out for the usual nasties first, you could talk me into it."

"Smile, big guy, you just came up with the only reason anyone would ever want AIDS."

Rantz responded with a sickening little smile, but he didn't hit and he didn't push closer and he didn't move his hand to any area more personal than the shoulder where it still rested. This was Rantz's version of a business call. It was time to find out what the business was.

"So what are you doing here, Rantz? Just checking up on me to see if I'm safe? You flatter me."

Rantz pulled back a little, doing his best to come up with a safe way to broach the subject.

"I hear you're working on the Wilsey case. I hear you're checking out all the sleaze he hung out with."

"Yeah? Where'd you hear that?"

"Didn't you hear we already nailed the Sarmiento kid?"

"Didn't you hear they let him go?"

"Who's paying you?"

"I don't have to tell you that, you know."

"Who's paying you, Noonan?"

He'd let me know what he wanted, and the power began to shift. He wouldn't be here if he didn't need something he thought I could give him. He leaned back and caught the glare of a streetlight on his face. The guy didn't have much of an upper lip, but what there was was covered in sweat. Whatever it was I was supposed to have, it looked like he needed it pretty badly.

"Call my lawyer."

I turned to leave, hoping I could end this little meeting on my terms. Rantz spun me around by the arm. His hand was up. If I hadn't been married to a cop, there was little doubt it would have landed across my face. Even so, I could tell I shouldn't push it.

"What do you want, Rantz? Do you want me to tell you I'm not working on the Wilsey thing? Do you really think I could get mixed up in something like this and go on with business as usual? You're supposed to be a smart guy, Rantz. You want to know if I'm working on Wilsey? Figure it out for yourself. You want to know if someone's paying? What difference does it make? You want to know what I've found out? You want to know if I think this involves cops? Or maybe blackmail? You want to know if this has anything to do with cops Wilsey knew were dirty? You tell me, Rantz. Tell me who was dirty. Tell me who was giving the guy money. Then we'll figure out who iced him together."

I must have guessed right. The sweat on his lip was actually beginning to roll down his face.

"You don't know shit."

"I'm willing to listen. Wilsey was dirty. Who else? What about Stub Kinnon? Were you at the precinct back then Rantz?"

"You're a smartass, just like your fucking husband Noonan."

"Ex-husband."

"Just back off, okay. You want this thing taken care of we'll take care of it. It's our job to find the guy who did the hit. Understand? Back off. Wilsey is ours."

"You mean yours?"

"I mean ours. And, listen, babe, just remember, I can take you in anytime I want. You want this case solved? Fine. You killed him. You shot him in the head."

"And why would I do that?"

"You two had been doing each other off and on the last ten years. Wilsey told me before he left the force. You think I don't know about the stuff you took out of Wilsey's apartment? Opium? I didn't know a cop's wife liked the freaky stuff. Is that why he dumped you, babe? Too strung out. What was it that made you kill the guy? He cut off your supply? Maybe he just upped his prices. I tell you sweetheart, you're in trouble. And there's nothing that drunk of a husband can do for you either."

He was back in control or at least he thought he was, wiping off his upper lip and sliding a cigarette under it. He made a point of not watching where he blew the smoke.

"And when I walk away from the whole thing?"

"By that time, babe, we'll have wrapped the whole thing up and put Wilsey to bed. So take your pick, darling. You can wait this thing out on the street with your new squeeze or you can make some new girlfriends in the nasty place. Think about it, sweetheart."

He knew he'd come up with something of an exit line, so he took advantage of it, blew one last stream of smoke into ny face, turned and headed off down the street. That left ne where? Police records for a start. Finding out just who vas at the precinct nine years back. Even if Rantz wasn't, he vas protecting someone who was. Was he dirty? Probably. At least, it made me glad to think he was.

It would make me feel even better if I could put Wilsey's nurder on Rantz. But if he'd done it, he wouldn't have nessed up with the first shot. And he probably wouldn't 1ave used a gun at all. A lethal overdose and no one would ven know the guy was murdered. So what did Rantz want? Time. Time to get Wilsey off everyone's mind.

The smell of Rantz's cigarette was still fresh in the air. The pressure from his hand had been such that it still felt as f he were holding on to my shoulder. It was a bet whether or not Rantz was bluffing. If he busted me and I walked, hings might not go so easy on him. Even so, I still wasn't ure I wanted a second visit.

For the first time, I noticed it had started to mist while Rantz was here. I ran my hand through my hair. It came up vet. The key to the building was still clamped tightly beween my fingers, ready to tear into Rantz's eyes. If the light vas better, I probably could have read the locksmith's name on the skin of my forefinger. I slipped the key into the lock und headed inside to try to sleep.

TWENTY-THREE

◆

It had been three days since I'd cleaned what was left of Wilsey from my apartment. I'd spent most of my time since then with users and sellers. Walking in neighborhoods where people couldn't help but notice me no matter how much I didn't want to be noticed. Finding out my ex-husband was a drunk. Not to mention getting threatened by cops and cop-lovers. I was sick of it all. Sick of Wilsey, sick of Frank, sick of having my dates topped off by visits from psychopaths, sick of the rain that hadn't let up for over a week, sick of my job, my life, and working on a case I wasn't getting paid for.

The time was ripe to revel in someone else's misery for a change, and I charged uptown to give Malcolm the information he wanted about the hussy who sat in Noah Lowell's class. I killed most of the morning tracking her down, putting a name to her body, finding out where she lived and what classes she took. I even got the chance to see her in action again. Batting her eyes at another professor as she handed in a late paper. Then I saw her rubbing up against this nerdy-looking grad-student type, trying to hustle him to write another one for her.

It was as sick and pathetic in its own way as everything else I'd experienced the last few days. Whoever Noah might be attracted to, he'd have nothing to do with a sicko like this. It was Malcolm's fault, my even having to think about her. One more reason to consider leaving. I took the obligatory pictures of the girl and left.

I had yet to make contact with Evie Weber, Wilsey's writing teacher, and it was looking increasingly important that I find out who was involved with Wilsey back when he was still on the force. Putting all that on hold till the afternoon so I could yell at Malcolm about his Hannah Lowell fiasco wouldn't help anything, but it wouldn't hurt either.

Only when I got to the office, the Malcolm I wanted to see wasn't the Malcolm I got. The Malcolm I'd psyched myself to lay into was the fat, pompous son of a bitch who let Hannah Lowell put me down, smirk in my face, anything just so he could take her money and get in her pants. In either order. He was the know-it-all boss who'd fought my partnership in the business for seven years, who'd delegated responsibility without delegating salary, who'd been trying to make me since the first time I'd walked in the office looking for a job. All those times I'd put off taking him down were finally coming due. The words would have something to do with company money, expensive presents, and cheap sluts.

That was the Malcolm I'd counted on confronting. That wasn't the one who'd shown up this morning. This Malcolm was pale and drawn. Where there was usually some life in his fleshy face, his skin seemed to sag lifelessly. He was slumped forward in his chair when I came in. Even though he'd been told to cut back on his caffeine, two cups of coffee sat on his desk. Next to them was the vial of pills that had become so familiar. He didn't even look up when I came in. He just popped another pill in his mouth and washed it down with a big slug of coffee. Good show, Rita. Fire away at the poor guy whenever you're ready.

"Malcolm. Are you okay?"

When he didn't respond at first, I took a step toward the phone. A trip to the hospital would be a perfect fit with this week.

"Are you okay?"

"Huh?"

"You scared the hell out of me. What's the matter with you?"

He turned and looked up at me vacantly.

"Rita. What are you doing here?"

"Jesus, Malcolm, you look like hell."

That probably wasn't what he needed to hear right now, but it didn't look like I'd get to lay into him right now, so I had to get in what I could. Malcolm didn't even seem to hear.

"I'm getting old."

He was talking, but not to me. Just putting words into the air, needing someone else to be there so they'd have some place to land.

"Watch what you eat. Okay? Watch what you drink. Okay? Watch out for too much . . ."

His eyelids closed heavily. Stubby little fingers pressed against them. His voice lowered several notches.

"I used to be able to . . . I used to . . ."

He hadn't said a word, really, and I was grateful for that. It was about sex. It had to be. Malcolm's whole life to this point had revolved around sex. Should he take a case? Would it get him laid? Should he hire a new assistant? Would it get him laid? Should he move to a nicer office? Would it get him laid?

Getting married had been a real quandary for him. Presumably, it fulfilled the obligatory requirement, but it also closed off other avenues of similar fulfillment. He'd muddled along until she left him. And mourned her loss until he asked the important questions. Did my wife leave me? Can it get me laid?

But he couldn't muddle now. Getting himself laid might also get him killed. His reason for being in the world was disappearing. His orientation was gone. He was lost. Like a Moonie waking up from deprogramming and wondering what he should do now.

"Hannah Lowell will kill me and I don't want to die. You wouldn't believe this woman, Rita. The things she does. The things she asks for. I've never met a woman like her. I've dreamed about her since I was six years old. Before that, probably. Now I meet her and . . ."

"And you spend half the company's money on her and nearly get yourself killed in the process."

I hadn't meant to say something like that. He wanted just to talk, hadn't even asked for sympathy. Maybe it was the implicit putdown. Being a woman and, as such, being compared to Hannah Lowell and coming up wanting wasn't the most pleasant way to start the morning. Maybe it was finding out one possible answer to the question what Noah Lowell ever saw in Hannah and finding that answer threatening. Whatever. Once these things are said, there's not much you can do about getting them unsaid.

Malcolm opened his eyes and slowly turned back to look at me.

"Hannah Lowell is a client here. We have an obligation to keep her happy."

"She's more than a client, Malcolm."

"And you've got a hell of a nerve talking about how we spend our money when you haven't done anything to make any for us lately. You can't even keep the cases I hand you."

Okay. So he was cornered and he attacked. I could understand that. There was no need to pick up his coffee and throw it in his face, no need to say the big two words and stalk out the door to open my own agency like I should have done six months ago when I'd had my name in the paper and all the attention I needed. No need at all. Just an incredible desire that could only be squashed by the realization that this wasn't six months ago and starting a new agency would be considerably more difficult now than it was then.

"You don't like how I work?"

"What work? You do nothing. Nothing."

"Fine. I'll remember that."

I threw my surveillance notes and the roll of film I took of the girl on his desk, picked up my coat, and headed out to call Max about some personnel files. The door shut. Behind me I could hear the ranting and raving continue. Lorenz, the accountant down the hall was unlocking the door to his office as the words "Don't come back, bitch" followed me down the hall. We both pretended not to notice.

TWENTY-FOUR

◆

I was shaking when I reached for the quarter to drop into the telephone at the restaurant across the street. It wasn't so much that I'd let Malcolm get to me. He'd gotten to me before. And I'd handled it before. And if I wanted to, I could handle it again right now. Only this time I was doing something about it.

I'd set out from the office with the sole purpose of burying myself in the Wilsey case. Calling Max at the precinct house. Digging further. I wanted to ignore my working situation. Ignore the fact that my partner was using company funds to finance his love affairs. Ignore the fact that he was too cheap to hire the right number of people or pay the people he did hire a living wage. Ignore the fact that anytime we sat down to discuss any of this he took it personally and laid into me about whatever fault of mine he felt would best deflect the criticism he had coming.

Only as I crossed the street and headed for the phone, I knew my call to Max was going to wait. I'd endured Malcolm's attitude for a good seven years in the hopes that some day he'd make me a partner. Then the day came, but the attitude just stayed the same. I was hearing the same garbage that I'd always heard and now there was nothing to look forward to.

"Hello, Henry Mencia, please."

I'd been carrying his phone number with me ever since he called. Tempted several times to throw it away, always hanging on to it just in case.

"Mr. Mencia, this is Rita Noonan of Ortner and Lloyd Investigations. I was hoping you'd still be interested in discussing the security position you mentioned earlier in the week."

Two minutes was all it took, and I had an appointment to see him for later that afternoon. Nothing to it. Simple. Direct. All it took for me to make the big bailout was a quarter. I hung up the phone and caught my breath before I made the next call.

Max was as eager to help me gather the personnel information I needed as I thought he'd be. It took seven different assurances that I'd never reveal where I got them, three promises that I wouldn't ask him to talk about any specific people, and the threat that without the information I'd be forced to turn what I did have over to a *Post* reporter I knew before he told me that he'd see what he could do. Even then, he wouldn't agree to meet me. If he could get the material, he'd get it to me. That was the least of the problems.

With that settled, I set off to finally meet with Evie Weber, fully anticipating that she might have no interest in sharing her insights with a woman who had so thoroughly alienated her employer. I tried to figure out if there was an honest way to do this sort of thing and, if there was, just what it would be. I was still working on it when I passed a pastry shop in Little Italy. I stepped inside, sat down at a small table, ordered sfogliatelle and a cup of espresso, and ate. Slowly.

I checked my notes. *Loisaida This Week* was the name of the paper where Evie Weber worked. A neighborhood rag. A relative of those uptown papers that existed primarily to provide writers a place to publish and local businesses an affordable place to advertise. The publishers got rich. Nobody read them. Everybody was happy.

Only *Loisaida This Week* was missing several crucial elements in the puzzle. Whatever small businesses managed to keep themselves alive in this neighborhood didn't have the money to waste on this kind of advertising and the most thriving business, drugs, found advertising, outside of word of mouth, tacky. On top of that, the paper's potential market consisted of about ten distinct language groups, and a significant percentage of those that did speak English were illiterate. That meant there was no money. That meant it was published collectively. That meant it existed solely to give the writers a place to put their words. Which meant that even those few people who might be able to read it wouldn't.

It was time to hit the street again to try to talk to one more person who probably didn't want to talk to me. And although I'd learned all sorts of ways to force people to provide me with information I needed, I decided to try a new one today. I bought a bag of pignoli-nut cookies. Hey, everybody loves a cookie and I just couldn't handle another angry face right now.

The offices of *Loisaida This Week* were just what I'd

imagined for a sixties-type alternative newspaper. A run-down tenement building. Walls full of yellowing posters about ending the war interspersed with newer ones protesting gentrification, homelessness, and racial violence. A bulletin board offering services ranging from dog-sitting and self-defense to immigration-rights classes and weaving lessons. It was college twenty years ago. Even the wardrobe brought back memories.

I spoke to a receptionist who spoke only Spanish but who managed to communicate that Evie Weber was in a staff meeting that had been going on for about an hour and a half and would soon be breaking up. I took a seat on a brightly painted park bench and began to thumb through a back-issue article lauding the new trend for dancers to use crack houses for rehearsal space. The dancers get free space. The dealers get a cover.

Just then, a door opened and a group of mostly jeans-clad people streamed out. The receptionist pointed to a slightly chubby attractive woman with long reddish-brown curly hair wearing a baggy black sundress over an oversized yellow T-shirt. She hustled out of the meeting, stopping at a small table to pick up a cup of coffee and some sort of sweet roll, then disappeared into the back-office area. I looked over to the receptionist to see whether I should buzz in, but she was involved with taking some sort of apartment listing from an Indian woman with a pit bull, so I just walked in.

The back offices were more of the same. Bright colors. Outdated office equipment. Desks, many without phones, separated only by a number of mismatched partitions. The effect seemed designed to encourage the workers to use their homes as much as possible. At least that was how I took it.

That must have been how Evie Weber took it also. By the time I found her cubbyhole, she was shoveling all sorts of papers into a tote bag, swallowing the last of her cup of coffee, and getting ready to leave.

"Evie Weber?"

Weber looked up, flashing this warm kind of smile you don't expect to see in New York.

"Yes."

I passed her my card, one of the few times I'd done that when I wasn't afraid it would come back to haunt me.

"I'm a private investigator. I'd like to ask you some questions about a student of yours."

"Rita Noonan? I'm not supposed to talk to you."

She wasn't belligerent. I hoped that meant something.

"I was afraid of that. Would you like a cookie?"

"Sure."

I offered her the bag of pignoli-nut cookies. She took out a couple, then looked again at my card.

"Private investigator, huh? Is it better than this?" She gestured to her surroundings.

"Not for the last week or so."

"Yeah, well, I just sat through a meeting where we had to talk for half an hour before we came to a consensus on how to ensure the constant presence of toilet paper in the bathroom. God, this cookie is to die for."

"Half an hour?"

She shook her head sadly. From around the corner this squat, solid guy with thick black curly hair and a matching thick black mustache appeared. He was the same guy Karl Marx had in mind when he first thought about working masses. Probably the only person in the world who actually considered himself part of that mass.

"Hey, Evie. They're holding a rally against that shooting in the Bronx on Friday. You want to go?"

"Sorry, Paul. I'm busy Friday."

"How about a movie sometime?"

"That would be nice."

"Terrific."

Then he disappeared. Probably to print up a leaflet and paste it to my building. Evie leaned forward.

"The movie's going to be some Cuban propaganda thing about record sugar production or something. Doesn't anybody just ask you out to dinner anymore? At a restaurant where they at least serve meat."

I hadn't felt good about my social situation in a long time. It still wasn't good. But it wasn't as bad as this woman's.

"You're going out with that guy?"

"No." She thought about it some more. "Unless, you know, it was a Friday night or something and my television was out. My mother always calls on Fridays. Just to make sure I'm doing something. I don't answer if I'm home. It's okay if I'm caught up in a show or something. But she lets that phone ring a long time. Can I have another cookie?"

I handed her the bag.

"So tell me who's this student of mine that warrants private investigation? And why am I not supposed to talk to you?"

"His name's Weiss. Wilsey Weiss."

"Wilsey? He was never exactly a student of mine."

"He wasn't?"

"No. I mean he came to me wanting to learn to write and everything. I work part-time for Placement Resources. Part-time at the New School. Part-time here. Part-time writing freelance articles. Part-time writing the perfect beach novel. Anything to pay for the apartment. I'm sorry, here I am eating all your cookies and I don't offer you anything. Do you want a cup of coffee?"

"I just had a cup of espresso before I came."

"Espresso? Jesus. Two cups of this stuff and I'm flying all day. Anyway, I get about three kinds of students. I get

the one with no writing skills who wants to learn just
enough to get this particular job. I get the one who needs
the credits to get some sort of degree. And then I get the
New School student who read somewhere that the course
was a good place to meet someone."

"Which one was Wilsey?"

"None. He had no intention of writing anything. He just
had this story. Excuse me. This great story. And if I would
write it for him, he'd guarantee it would be a bestseller and
he'd cut me in for a percentage."

"Did you do it?"

Evie just arched her eyebrows and looked at me like I was
crazy.

"Did he tell you what it was about?"

"Something about cops, corruption, drugs, the usual."

"But there was no book?" I asked.

"Not that I saw."

"And that was it?"

"No. He'd come to my classes, sit there without listening,
then charge the desk afterward with some great idea he was
sure would change my mind. It lasted about a month and a
half. Why are you asking?"

"Wilsey's dead. He was shot in my apartment."

I'd figured Goenther had already told her about Wilsey
but apparently he hadn't. The color drained quickly from
her cheeks. A sudden shudder shook her body. I hadn't
played fair with the Wilsey thing. I'd sprung the death thing
out of nowhere and she'd taken it hard, so I figured why not
tell her what I knew. It sometimes helped.

"Do you think there was someone else who might have
taken him up on his offer?"

"You mean another writer? Who knows. But you knew
the guy. Would you cut a deal like that with him? Banking
six months of your life on a true story you probably couldn't

verify and that he could be making up off the top of his head. The funny thing is . . ."

"Yes?"

"Under the circumstances, I kind of wish I'd done it now."

It wasn't ghoulish, just practical. I handed her another card, one with my home number written on it, told her to call me if she thought of anything, and that was that. No threats, no accusations, no violence. Just a little information over coffee and cookies. The civilized way to investigate. I could learn to love this career all over again.

TWENTY-FIVE

♦

The message on my machine was a long one. And Rafe's voice was familiar, even over a pay phone whose receiver looked as if it could have been the mysterious blunt instrument used by some still unapprehended killer. Rosa Sarmiento had called the office. She was worried. Her husband had left home this morning but had never shown up for work and the police hadn't picked him up and she didn't know where he was. She left her address.

There was more. Malcolm hadn't felt well and had gone home early, and Rafe wanted me to know he was sorry for the hard time he'd given me the other day. Peg had come back. She'd give him some more time with the job, although she wasn't too crazy about his working so closely with a woman who found dead bodies in her apartment. There was still more to talk about, but there was only so much he

could say to a machine and besides he wasn't sure if most of
the message hadn't already been cut off.

Visiting Rosa Sarmiento's apartment was about the last
thing I wanted to do right now. There was still plenty of
time before I had to meet Mencia, but I'd planned to spend
it picking out more suitable clothes than those I was wearing. An old sweater of Frank's I'd never had the heart to
throw out, a pair of jeans and some sneakers. The outfit had
seemed perfect this morning when I set off for Columbia.
What I needed now was some sexless blue suit that would
give me corporate credibility.

I could've gone home and picked up the snappy little
number my aunt had bought me when I'd graduated from
high school and she figured I'd be heading for secretarial
school. I could even break down and pop for something
new. Only now it looked like I'd be staying in the Lower
East Side, where corporate blue suits were tough to find and
wearing one might get me killed. It would be safer to take
my chances with Mencia, telling him I'd spent the day on
some sort of stakeout. Who knows, he might even get a kick
out of it.

Rosa Sarmiento's apartment was in a building roughly
equivalent to the one Wilsey had lived in, on a block full of
the same abandoned buildings, vacant lots, and strung-out
junkies. The front lock had been pulled out. The usual
words and pictures were spray-painted inside and out. The
usual smells permeated everything. It was the kind of building of which there seemed to be no shortage in Manhattan.
Filthy. Run-down. And if the developers could get their
hands on it, the apartments would be going for three hundred thousand per.

It was hard to imagine Rosa Sarmiento still being worried
about anything regarding her husband. So he was late. How
late had he been when they'd arrested him and put him in

jail? He wasn't at work either. Somehow, the difficult part for me to believe was that he ever made it there at all. And yet Rosa Sarmiento had never called me to look for her husband before. There must be something more.

She opened the door to a third-floor walk-up. Wearing a faded dark blue dress, the woman still looked twice as old as the age she was supposed to be. The apartment went with the sense of wear she exuded. The furniture was worn. Dark, heavy fabrics. Thick, worn rugs. Bulbs burning so yellow, everything looked shabbier than it was. Even the little girl standing in the doorway to a back bedroom had the same tired eyes as her mother.

"Did he come back yet, Mrs. Sarmiento?"

There was always the off chance that he had and I'd just wasted my trip. Rosa Sarmiento shook her head.

"What happened?"

"He come home yesterday. He say he talk to you. He say Wilsey dead because he know too much. He say he have idea. Maybe he can know too much, too. He say maybe he can make something of this, maybe he can find out what Wilsey knew or maybe pretend Wilsey tell him, maybe he can work something out."

She was saying he'd left to blackmail someone and never came home. She was also saying he'd done it because of something I'd said.

"Did he say who he was going to talk to?"

The woman shook her head.

"Did he say where he was going?"

"Maybe Wilsey."

"Is there anything more you can tell me?"

The woman thought. There couldn't have been much of a life to salvage with this man, yet there were still red eyes and sagging shoulders. Whatever had happened before, this time she seemed to have already begun mourning the guy.

"Bobby always a little crazy, lady. He want to deal the drugs. Make money. That all he want. All he ever want."

I turned to leave.

"You find Bobby. You bring him home."

There were a lot of places Bobby could be and a lot of people he could have tried to blackmail, and I only had one clue to work with. I couldn't even assume he'd be going after the same people Wilsey had worked on because, from everything Rosa had told me, he'd had no idea Wilsey had ever been blackmailing anyone. Unfortunately for Bobby, that one clue was all I needed.

I got to Wilsey's building in the late afternoon, and the first thing I noticed was how quiet it all was. The cowboy was gone. There was no guardian at the gate.

I pushed the front door open. Inside, it was the same. Quiet. No muffled screaming and shouting from behind anonymous closed doors. Not even from Bina's. And there wasn't any music coming in from outside. It was like everyone had gone to the country for the day or maybe the immigration people had decided to pay a visit.

I knocked on Bina's door. It would be worth the fifty bucks not to have to break into Wilsey's apartment. It'd probably be worth even more not to go up there alone. Much to my surprise, there was no answer.

I climbed the steps, not looking forward to another tour through Wilsey's apartment. Breaking in, this time, even if it had to be under the watchful eyes of the skeevy character from the opium den upstairs. Where would he be? In the bathtub. Pushed out the window. Chopped up and stuffed in the cupboards.

Only Bobby had been a lot more cooperative than that. Not only had he gone right where he'd said he would, he didn't even make me look for him once I got here. He was lying faceup on the floor of the hallway. Propping Wilsey's door open. If the killer was the same person who had shot Wilsey, his practice had definitely had an effect. There'd been no need for a second shot this time. The one little hole in the center of his forehead had done the job quite nicely.

I looked up the stairs. The skeevy guy was gone. No sickening smile as he checked me out. I made the obligatory check of Wilsey's apartment, knowing all along I wouldn't find anything. Then I went upstairs.

I'd never come up here before, so I'd never know exactly what had changed. Whatever it was, the place was now stripped bare. The traveling opium den had packed up and gone. Opening up again no doubt in some location I'd only find out about if I began to travel in a society far more exclusive than the one I currently traveled in. There was no carpet, no curtains, no chairs. Or couches, or lamps, or anything. Only the smell stayed behind. Pretty soon that would get swallowed by the more powerful human smells that owned the rest of the building. My footsteps echoed as I walked back downstairs.

TWENTY-SIX

◆

I made the call to the cops about Bobby Sarmiento anonymously from a phone booth on the corner of First Street and Avenue A. The wind had picked up, pushing through the corridors between buildings that the streets provided. The sky was still overcast. The little bit of rain that was still in the air whipped around so hard it stung. It was early May. In a couple of weeks everyone would be crying about the ninety-degree weather and the high humidity. For now, it was a Canadian cold front and a stalled low-pressure system that was doing the damage.

Theoretically, I should have stayed with the body, watching all the funny things that happened to it as it turned cold. I should have hung around that rank, filthy building so I could provide the cops with all my insights as to what Bobby was doing there, who might have killed him, or why he was killed. And I'm sure they'd be interested in what I was doing there as well.

Only I didn't have any of the answers they were looking for, not unless I concurred with Rosa Sarmiento, who blamed the whole thing on me. I'd grown sick of this building long ago and I'd already been tied too closely with one body this week. Besides, if I put myself through their question-and-answer session just now, I'd never make it to the Mencia appointment. Let the cops figure this one out for themselves. I hung up the phone and figured I had just enough time to break the news to Rosa and her kid with the tired eyes. For some reason, I assumed they'd already be wearing black when I got there.

TWENTY-SEVEN

◆

All the way down to Mencia's office I kept thinking about how Sarmiento's dying changed things. It didn't necessarily destroy Morris and Rantz's case. Who's to say the guy who killed Wilsey couldn't get killed himself. It wasn't as if committing murder would give Sarmiento a free pass for the rest of his life. And his murder wouldn't necessarily have anything to do with Wilsey's. Maybe the guy had just over-played his hand following up on an idea he'd gotten from talking to a screwball private investigator.

Be that as it may, Sarmiento's getting killed would at least cause some rethinking. There'd be the ballistics test, of course. Checking to see if the same gun that killed Wilsey was used to kill Sarmiento. Either way the test went, the story would almost have to get more complicated. No more simple junkie argument taking place during the middle of a burglary. If it was the same gun, who had it now? If there were two guns, did the third person come in after the fact or had he been along for the ride from the beginning? Now they'd have to ask, why my apartment? Why now? What were they looking for? Why? There hadn't been much to steal. And what there was was still there. They'd have to ask about the books. They'd have to look for new suspects. I hoped that didn't mean I should expect another of Rantz's midnight calls.

Whatever this meant to Rantz and Morris, I for one was crossing Sarmiento off the suspect list. I'd never been too crazy about the burglary bit. My bet was, Sarmiento had never set foot in my apartment. But someone had. And the only reason that came to mind was one that didn't make sense—the books Wilsey planted in my apartment to cover for the one I'd yet to find. And that looked more and more like the one I needed to find if I hoped to find Wilsey's killer. The one I hoped Bobby Sarmiento hadn't found. I was almost tempted to go back to Wilsey's apartment for another search, but it was too late for that now.

I wanted to talk to Nell again. Imaculata she'd said her name was. Sounded like a stage name to me. And she'd never given out her real one. That meant leafing through the phone book on the off chance she listed herself as such. If

not, I could call all the theatrical agencies to see if I could
reach her that way, but that was assuming she had some
sort of representation. After that, it was skip-trace work.
Tracking her down by accessing any and all information I
could find. God knows, I hoped she was as famous as she
thought she was.

It wasn't until I'd actually walked into the prewar
building where Mencia's office was located that I began
to think about what I was doing and wonder if I really
wanted to be here. I'd spent too many years already in
dead-end jobs, some corporate, some not. Waitress. Parale-
gal. Proofreader. Part-time department-store cashier at Christmas. There was even a security stint in the women's dressing
room at a tony clothiers. No money. No benefits. Spending
most of the day thinking up creative new ways to complain
about my life.

I figured it was all part of working for someone else and
swore I'd never work in a large operation again. That's
when the whole idea of investigation came up. Surveillance.
Something I could do on my own pretty much. I would
never have taken the job with Malcolm except that I needed
to learn the business somehow and New York laws required
too much experience for me just to go out and pick up a
license of my own.

That was how it started. I'd gone over the idea of quitting
many times over the last few years, especially since I'd
established a level of competence I felt comfortable with.
And every time I'd found that the reasons to stay out-
weighed the ones to leave.

Only here I was. It was after six. The lobby was pretty
much empty. The night man at the desk had shown up, but
he wasn't making anyone sign in just yet. I looked around.
The lobby was a far cry from the neighborhoods I'd just
come from. The marble floors and walls sparkled, the

handiwork of an army of cleaning-service specialists. The ceiling rose at least two stories, with some huge old chandeliers that looked like they'd come from an old movie house. Even the lettering in the directory was neat and up-to-date. It was all so clean. And right now that impressed me.

Mencia's office was small. Just a front desk for a receptionist-secretary and an inner office for him. In today's world it would be called a boutique. But even if it was small, the place was anything but shabby. Solid oak front door, thick plush carpeting, original artwork on the wall. Mencia met me at the door.

"I'm sorry my secretary isn't here. She had to leave early. Knicks playoff tickets."

He smiled warmly, but professionally. The guy was younger than he'd sounded on the phone. Designer suit. Designer hair. Designer tortoiseshell glasses. All designed to make him seem like the casual king of the Western world.

"I would have liked to dress better. I was on a case."

"That's all right. In fact, it's terrific. Another murder?"

"As a matter of fact."

I'd left Bobby Sarmiento's body less than an hour and a half ago and already he was just cocktail-party conversation. Worse than that, he'd become part of my résumé. More impressive than any case I'd worked on. Somehow, if someone died, things just seemed more important.

We walked into Mencia's office. There was more original artwork and a mahogany desk whose construction must have required most of a rain forest. Aside from a couple of chairs, the only other item in the room was a computer. This was a man who clearly knew what the good life was and how to get it. And out of the goodness of his heart, he was willing to show me how to get the good life, too. Only it didn't feel right.

In fact, the whole of Mencia's questioning didn't sit right.

He asked about my experience with computers. Most corporate investigative work revolves primarily around gathering and sorting electronic information. But when I said I knew next to nothing about them, he only shrugged and said that will give the people who work for you something to do. He didn't ask about cases I'd worked on or references I could offer. What he wanted was stories, the more violent or perverse the better.

"They're going to love you, Rita. I swear. This stuff is great."

The fact that it was also people's lives didn't seem to bother him in the least. And it obviously hadn't bothered me enough to keep those stories to myself.

We talked for a half an hour before he turned to his computer screen and called up three security jobs he thought I might qualify for. The worst of them paid more than twice what I was making now. That was before the benefits, the vacations, the bonuses.

It was a world to which I'd never had access. The people I'd be working with had never been near an office like Malcolm's. If they needed help, they went to the larger outfits. Even if I'd still be looking on the dark side of things, it would be a lighter shade of dark. Nothing of what he said changed the fact that what he felt I had to offer was something along the lines of a freak show. Still, at those prices, a freak show might have a certain appeal.

TWENTY-EIGHT

◆

I hadn't given Mencia an answer. I'd left telling him I'd think it over. Playing it cool, mostly. But I also didn't want to do something like this on a whim. There'd be no looking back once I'd gone. Only all the way home I couldn't think of one reason to do anything but take the job, get down on my knees, and shout hallelujah.

This was the kind of time meant to be celebrated with close friends. Right now friends were in short supply. Malcolm of course was off-limits. So was Frank. That pretty much left Noah, and he was still practically a stranger. Besides, how would I explain the whole detective thing to him? I headed back to my empty apartment swearing to myself that I wouldn't call some half-dead aunt out in Pocatello, Idaho, just to have someone to tell. Sometimes good news had a way of really bringing me down.

I checked my mail and Max had been there. A copy of the police personnel files at Wilsey's precinct during his tour of duty was in an unmarked plain white envelope. No note accompanied them. I'm sure if the thing had been dusted for fingerprints I would have found that Max had worn gloves.

I climbed up the stairs, leafing through the reports and figuring just how I was going to track down Nell Imaculata tomorrow. I looked up to see a woman standing in front of my door. Blond. Good figure. Wearing a raincoat that couldn't hide it.

"I want to know why you're sleeping with my husband."

Carla's voice was flat, even, with a slight accent that betrayed her Brooklyn origins. Whatever anger there was was subdued. Like she'd done this too many times before to be giving it her best effort.

"I'm not sleeping with Frank."

What else was there to say? It was the truth. She could either believe me or not believe me.

"He admitted he was."

"Then he's lying."

Carla stood there at the door. She might have looked stupid except it was way too easy to put myself in her position. We were standing next to each other. Carla wasn't exactly looking me in the eye. She wasn't crying. There were no shudders or shivers. But she wasn't leaving either. Whatever she'd thought might happen on her way over here must have played a lot better in her head.

"Do you want to come in?"

Carla looked at me strangely. When she didn't answer, I put the key in my lock and went inside. Carla followed.

"He hasn't been coming home a lot from work. And when I come home, he leaves."

"I don't envy you."

She was looking around at this place, at my bed, imagining Frank here, imagining the life we must have had together. "Awkward" was the word that came to mind.

"He talks about you a lot. Then I saw you at our home the other day. I just thought . . ."

"I'm a private investigator now. I came to see him about a case I'm working on."

"That's what Frank told me, but he's told me a lot of stuff before and very little of it turned out to be true. I never went to see any of the other women. This just didn't seem fair. What did you think, that it didn't count because you used to be married to the guy or something? I mean, you had your turn. You knew what this was all about. You knew how it felt. I just wanted to let you know it still feels that way."

Carla'd said she believed me, but she'd just delivered the speech she'd practiced on the way over, so I figured she still needed some convincing. I wasn't doing it for myself and God knows I wasn't trying to save Frank's ass. But Carla was still upset. It wouldn't hurt her to know there was at least one woman her husband was not sleeping with.

I told her about how I was working on a murder involving someone we'd both known when we were married, an ex-cop, who'd suddenly come back into my life. Then he'd been killed. I spared Carla the part about where he got killed. She was uncomfortable enough about being here already. I explained that I'd turned to Frank only to find out if he knew anything about the guy, if he knew why he might want to get in touch, anything.

"Believe me, Carla, it's not fun for me either."

As the story'd gone on, I could tell Carla was letting herself be convinced.

"Who was the guy?"

"His name was Wilsey."

"Wilsey?"

"You knew him?"

"No. I mean, yeah. I knew who he was. Frank ran into him every once in a while."

"Recently?"

I'd tried not to show too much interest, but the question stood for itself. I waited while Carla deliberated just how much allegiance she owed right now to Frank. When she finally spoke, her words came slowly and completely without emotion.

"The last time I know for sure was about a year ago. We stopped at this apartment on the Upper East Side. Frank had to drop something off with the guy on our way to this show someone had given us tickets to. He wouldn't even go up. He just rang the buzzer. This Wilsey character came down. Frank gave him whatever, then got in the car and that was that."

This was the first time I'd seen her crying. It wasn't sobs or anything. Just tears.

"Do you want a drink or something?"

"I don't drink."

"What are you going to do?" I asked.

"I don't know."

I'd wanted to dislike the woman since before I'd ever seen her. It wasn't jealousy, at least not in any way that implied I wanted Frank back and she was standing in the way. Comparisons were more the problem. Not where I stood. Just being compared at all. But now, while we'd still never be great friends, she just seemed too numb already for me to want to hurt her any more.

"You know," she said, talking more to herself than to me, "the first time I caught Frank in one of these little things of his, he told me it was a problem for him. He told me it had already nearly ruined his life. He told me he'd started therapy right after you'd divorced him and that he was still seeing that person and that he was still working on it. Something about fear of getting close and self-destructive behavior. It didn't sound like Frank and all. And he was crying. And I gave him another chance. And then another. And another. And now this time he didn't do anything, and for some reason I don't think I can take it anymore. Does that sound strange to you?"

She wasn't looking for a reply. She just got up and walked to the door.

"Thanks. I'm sorry I bothered you."

She left. Taking with her most of what I'd ever figured to

be true about my former husband. He'd been lying about Wilsey. Not only had he been seeing him, he'd been delivering things to him. Was he one of the cops who'd been paying him on the side? For what? What would Frank have to cover up? What about his straight-ahead, report-anything-that-comes-his-way attitude? What had Frank done?

But even there I could imagine something, some reason, some one slip in the course of his entire career that he'd regretted and had paid for for the rest of his life. Even Frank was human. Would it have been money? A woman? What would it take to turn Frank around? I'd never thought it could happen, but apparently it did.

The part that was so tough to figure was the therapy thing. Frank. That meant a psychiatrist. Only that couldn't be Frank. Not on his own. And she'd said it was the breakup of our marriage that had sent him there. Frank. He'd never even said he was sorry about his affairs. He'd just laughed them off. They hadn't meant anything, so why worry about them? Only how much laughing could he have been doing if he'd gone running to a psychiatrist as soon as I'd left him.

It was all too much to believe. Maybe he'd just made up the shrink story to get her off his back. But whether any of it was true or not, Frank was beginning to get his way. Worming himself back into my mind, getting me to think about him as if it still mattered. And I hated it.

I had work to do. There were the files to look through. And I had to track Nell down. I should even start thinking about what to do about the job interviews Mencia wanted to set up.

TWENTY-NINE

♦

I woke up the next morning having learned more old and useless information about the police than I knew what to do with, while having learned nothing about Nell other than that she wasn't listed in the phone book under the name she gave me. I wasn't sure what I'd expected to find in the personnel files Max had brought me. There was information about awards and commendations. I learned about which cops seemed to take an inordinate number of sick days. There were arrest statistics. Details about injuries received in and out of the line of duty. Even information about individual officers' faults and idiosyncrasies.

What there wasn't was a list of all the cops who were on the take. There was no detailed information of who was taking how much from whom. I recognized several names of people who were still around, such as Frank and Max and Rantz and Morris. There were another bunch who had since retired, and presumably would not be threatened by whatever it would be that Wilsey could reveal. There were also three or four whom I knew had died. Wilsey, of course, and Stub Kinnon, and a kid named Babcock who was killed in a hit-and-run by a drunken housewife while on his way home from a Mets game. But, even for Wilsey, there was no red-ink stamp informing whoever was supposed to look at these things that the guy was dirty. If I was going to find out anything about these guys, someone would have to tell me.

I'd pretty much decided to at least pursue Mencia's offer

as far as the interview stage, but I wasn't up to telling Malcolm about it quite yet. That meant putting off the office. And right now that also meant a little more research and heading uptown to my favorite research librarian at the New York Public Library.

Roger Gold was a man whose mere existence was enough to give credence to the whole idea of fate. With his balding head, his wire-rimmed glasses and his slightly retiring personality, he was born only to the world of books. Not once in the many years I'd turned to him for help had he worn anything but tweed. He belonged in the library like he'd belong nowhere else, and he knew it. He wasn't particularly superior to the other research specialists, but he seemed to thrive on whatever challenges I could hand him, as though finding the information I needed was his way of taming whatever chaos ruled his own life. Maybe there was something wrong about taking advantage of a man's neuroses as often as I did Roger's. While I waited for him to come back with everything he could find on Nell Imaculata's life story, I decided to put off worrying about it.

Roger handed me a pile of magazines, then leaned forward over his desk and whispered conspiratorially, "This is what I found to start with, but there's an intriguing little reference to an underground movie called *EAT* that we might want to track down if you don't find what you're looking for here."

He almost seemed to wink at me as I thanked him and headed over to a desk to check out the dirt.

Once again Roger had done himself proud. In the fourth article he gave me, there was a list of the whole stable of Bucinski actors. Nell's name was Nell Weston. She was the daughter of a steel executive named Burt Weston. Burt Weston lived in Bronxville, New York.

It couldn't have fit more beautifully. The two busts Wilsey

had had outside the city. What had he done? Gone out for a visit, met the folks, and robbed the neighbors? Maybe he'd been real ambitious and robbed the family. It was Wilsey right down the line. Screwy. And from what I'd seen of Nell, it had probably been her idea.

There was still no Nell Weston listed in the phone book. But there was a Burt Weston, in an apartment on the Upper East Side.

I wanted to run up right away and check if my hunch was right, but it was time to head back downtown. Malcolm would be there. I had to tell him about the interviews. For some reason it didn't sound like as much fun as I'd thought it would be. It would mean the end of the agency. Malcolm would never promote Rafe, and he wasn't healthy enough to train someone else like he'd trained me. That's why he'd made me a partner. If I left, it would all be over. How was I supposed to tell him that? I hadn't figured it out by the time I got there, but a couple of beers probably wouldn't hurt.

When he saw the beers, Malcolm looked up suspiciously. "What happened?"

"Nothing, Malcolm. I just thought we could have a beer."

I handed him the bottle and he opened it. He was still suspicious, but that only meant he might not want to take the beer if he waited till after we talked.

"You never followed up on that girl in the pictures, did you? You got caught up in that stupid fucking dead guy and you dropped the case that's making us money. Hannah was right. She said you were nothing but trouble, and . . ."

He took a sip of the beer, aware that he'd said more than he'd wanted to, wondering how long it would be before I'd ask exactly what Hannah Lowell said and what her opinion had to do with anything. He waited until he realized this wouldn't be the time.

"This isn't about the girl, Malcolm."

"Oh."

"I got a phone call the other day. A man named Mencia."

"You got a case? What kind of case? If it's another missing-persons thing, we're too busy."

"It's not a case, Malcolm. He's a headhunter. He finds people to work for major corporations. He fills openings."

"I know what a headhunter is."

"He said he could find me a job. Head of security. Security and information services. I'd be managing a whole staff of uniforms and data processors. Over eighty thousand a year plus benefits."

Malcolm didn't say anything for a minute. He rubbed his eyes, suddenly exhausted.

"You know, if you leave me, I'm through."

"I thought about that."

"What are you going to do?"

"I don't know."

"I think we could grow here. Really. I've been thinking about this, Rita. What we need is a face person. Someone to bring in the big clients. The ones we don't get. I was think-ing of asking Hannah. Just for a couple of cases. The kind you've been talking about. Then if we get them, maybe we could do something a little more permanent with her."

I didn't ask why we needed her, or what was wrong with my face. I didn't even suggest any ideas of permanent things we could do with her. But there didn't seem to be much more to say either, and it wouldn't do to just sit there staring at the floor, the ceiling, and anything else in the office that wasn't Malcolm all day.

"I just thought you should know."

I left.

THIRTY

♦

I walked over to the subway to go uptown to Nell's, taking time only to check in with my phone machine. I tried not to use the remote much. I figured I could wait to get home to listen to a computer rattle on about a special limited opportunity especially designed for me, Rita Noonan, to buy land in the Poconos that could only rise in value. But who knew? Maybe when I got to my machine, I'd have a message from Jesus Rantz: "I can't take it anymore. You're too good a detective. It was too much pressure. I killed Wilsey Weiss. And now I'm going to kill myself. I lost. You were just too good for me."

Only Jesus Rantz hadn't called. Noah Lowell had. He had some news and wanted to see me. Tonight. His voice was rushed, as if he wanted to make sure the message got through before he got beeped off. He'd be at the same restaurant for dinner. At seven. And this time he'd be early. Then he started to laugh, and that's when he did get beeped.

I waited for more. But there were no confessions. That was fine. I'd settle for another dinner with Noah. For a start. Then I'd find out who killed Wilsey. I'd get the new job. I'd live to one hundred, and find out in heaven that Mel Gibson should have married me and God would give him to me for the rest of eternity to make up for the mistake. I got on the subway.

Burt Weston's apartment was in a new building in the East Eighties. There was nothing quaint about the building or the block it sat on. There were no cute little townhouses that cost millions but still allowed their owners to proclaim their down-home values. There were no trees on the sidewalk either, planted and maintained by some maniacal block committee. Instead, there were high-rises and plazas, signposts that this block was about money. Rather than a neighborhood watch, there was an armed security officer. All to take the city out of city living.

The address in the phone book put the Weston apartment at No. 357, a towering black-mirrored building just off the corner. Inside were both a doorman and another character whose role, outside of greeting people, was hard to determine. Unlike the doorman, he wore no uniform and he certainly had no intention of performing any service as mundane as opening a door or helping with a package. And from the looks of the guy, he wouldn't be much help if there was trouble on the block either. What he had was a smile, a haircut, some clothes, and probably a college education. All so visitors wouldn't have to deal with an accent when he asked them their name and who they were going to see. The jerk probably took the lion's share of the Christmas tips.

"Nell Weston, please."

"And who shall I say is calling?"

There was no trace of an accent, not even one of the acceptable ones. The guy smiled the same genuine, warm smile I was used to seeing in commercials.

"Rita Noonan. I met her at her friend Wilsey's earlier in the week."

"Just a moment."

He made a phone call from a discreet distance away, speaking so quietly that there was no way for me to eavesdrop. I wondered if maybe there was a school where you learned this sort of thing.

"Miss Weston seemed a bit surprised, but she'd be delighted to see you. Thirty-six E."

The elevators were larger than my apartment and better decorated. The halls were lit with carefully positioned indirect fixtures and carpeted with a rug so thick I could feel my feet sink into it with every step. I wondered how much I'd have to pad that résumé to get one of the jobs Mencia had talked about.

The door to 36-E was open when I got there. I stood in the doorway and looked directly out through an enormous picture window at a view of the East River and the Queensboro Bridge. Not much to look at when you were down next to them, maybe, but from here they looked fine.

The rest of the apartment did its best to match the view. Ceilings so high they made no economic sense whatsoever. Wood floors I could see my reflection in. Original works of art on the walls, some by artists I could name. Furniture they didn't sell at Macy's, most of it appearing to have been custom-made to sit just where it did. They'd probably have to call the decorator in for an emergency session if they ever felt like rearranging the living room.

I tried to figure how Nell fit into all this. And maybe twenty or thirty years ago it would have been difficult—the high-wired speed freak in the secondhand clothes lying burned out in a rat-infested apartment when she had all this at her fingertips. But I'd seen and heard enough about this kind of thing so that the only news could be the distance of the disparity. Come to think of it, it was probably the same story back then, too.

Nell came in suddenly from a back room wearing nothing but a towel, her hair pulled back so severely it must have hurt. She walked forcefully, with the same sense of urgency that informed her movements the first time I'd seen her.

Only now the jerkiness was gone. There were no speed spasms. She appeared to be flying on regular, at least for the moment.

"I was in the shower when you rang. I'm sorry to make you wait."

The words still came quickly but, again, down several notches from what her voice was before.

"That's all right. I wanted to update you on Wilsey."

"Sure. Just a minute."

She turned and ran back to the bedroom, returning a moment later with an armful of clothes, none of which looked secondhand in the least.

"I'm supposed to meet my father for cocktails downtown at six and he'll kill me if I'm late. You don't mind."

I wasn't sure what I wasn't supposed to mind until she dropped the wet towel over the arm of an antique silk chair, leaving herself standing there naked while I was supposed to question her. She was thin like only someone who'd been taking speed for years could be and beginning to sag here and there. She looked like something small that was supposed to shiver when it got this exposed only she didn't.

"What did you find?"

"I was wondering if you could tell me first how you met the guy."

She was slipping into a pair of silk tap pants, the kind they sold in Victoria's Secret catalogues but that seemed a little too much to qualify as underwear.

"We were in detox together. Daddy would have died if he'd known where I was. He'd much prefer to see me at some celebrity clinic, but, my God, that would have been boring. No, I was living with some friends in the East Village and we all decided to give it up at the same time on a bet. I faked my name and got into a clinic program run by some nuns, you know. Then we both dropped out at the same time and we've been together on and off ever since."

It was the kind of story they would have told their grand-children if only Wilsey hadn't bought it. I did my best to keep from getting choked up as Nell was now throwing on a cashmere sweater that even felt soft from where I was standing.

"Did he know about your money?"

"I don't have any money. My parents do, of course, and he met them. He tried to steal half a dozen of my mother's furs, too, that jerk. Some good impression, huh? But I don't have a dime. My father cut me off a long time ago," she said as she wriggled into a matching cashmere skirt.

"Did you know many of his friends?"

Nell shrugged. "Some, I guess."

"Bobby Sarmiento?"

"Sure, Bobby. But I never trusted him. He was always getting Wilsey in trouble. It seems like every time they went out together, Wilsey got caught. In fact, if I had to guess, I wouldn't be surprised if Bobby did it. That's the kind of guy he is. What a temper."

"He's dead."

"Bobby?"

"He was in Wilsey's apartment. Shot in the head."

I was being a little abrupt, but there was something about the way the woman dealt with drug addiction and murder as items on her social calendar that made me want to shake her up a little.

"Oh, that poor boy. He was so ambitious, you know. Always trying to better himself and everything. He thought he could become this big-time dealer just because he wanted to be. He just didn't want to work for it. Of course, he came from overseas, so that explains a lot. We told him if he kept pushing so hard, sooner or later he'd get into trouble. Do they know who did it?"

I shook my head.

"Isn't it crazy? All these people dying so close together and everything. It almost gives me the creeps."

Nell hiked up her panty hose and slipped her feet into some soft leather Italian jobs that no doubt had been hand-crafted to fit her high arches.

"You weren't there when Bobby died, were you? You didn't see anything? Hear anything? Talk to anyone?"

"Nothing and no one. Daddy and I had a long talk after Wilsey died. I was all alone, of course, with no place to go and no money. We had this terrific rapprochement. He's going to help me again and I'm going to get cleaned up. This time he gets to pick the program."

Nell rolled her eyes as if to say parents can be so silly.

"And you never found Wilsey's book?"

Nell just looked at me for a moment, then shook her head and smiled sadly.

"Let's just face the facts. Wilsey could never write a book, could he?"

Apparently, that was all Nell had time for. She looked at the antique clock on the onyx mantel over the fireplace, and ushered me out on her way to meet her father at his downtown club.

It was raining again when we reached the street, but there wasn't even time for one drop to hit Nell's head between the time she left the shelter of the awning and the moment she got into the cab that miraculously appeared.

"Thanks so much for dropping by. Really. And do keep in touch."

THIRTY-ONE

♦

"I just got a job offer from Wisconsin. Full-time. Associate professor. They even want me to continue in my field, phenomenological approaches to film studies. I'd have to teach introductory film theory, too, of course, but they want me to continue with the original work."

I hadn't been sure what Noah's news was going to be. I was just flattered he'd wanted to share it with me. I'd run a few possibilities through my head, of course. There was the obligatory scenario that he'd fallen head over heels in love with me and couldn't wait even a moment to see me again. I noted the idea and dismissed it. By the time I'd arrived at the restaurant, I'd settled on one scenario where he'd found out I was a detective who'd been hired by his wife to report on him and a second where he'd won the lottery, but I wasn't quite sure how I figured into that picture.

What I wasn't prepared for was to hear that Noah was leaving. Why was I suddenly wishing I was back on the Lower East Side tripping over bodies? This was not what I wanted to be hearing right now.

"Wisconsin?"

"They've got a strong department."

"Are you going to take it?"

I deliberately leaned over to grab a dumpling with my chopsticks so Noah wouldn't be able to read anything into the question.

"I've got no choice."

No one in Wisconsin had ever offered me a job, but if they did, I was sure I'd have a choice. I waited for him to explain it to me.

"Do you know how long I've been an adjunct? Seven years. Seven years of low pay. No benefits. No security. The colleges invented it to fill in a course here and there that their full-time staff couldn't cover and fell in love with it. Not paying people has an amazing way of improving the bottom line. Wisconsin is a dream job."

So now I understood why he wanted to go to Wisconsin. That still left question number two.

"Why are you telling me this?"

The question was more direct than Noah looked like he'd been expecting. A huge smile passed across his face, then a laugh, then he shook his head.

"Well, I guess I was thinking I'd like to know what it would be like going out with you for about the tenth time, and the only way I'm going to find out now is to hurry to get two through nine out of the way."

It was a better line than telling me he wanted to make sure he got to sleep with me before he left. Which, when I thought about it, wouldn't be the worst thing in the world, but wouldn't have gotten him anywhere. In fact, it was the kind of line I could fall for in a big way.

Only what was it supposed to mean? Did this mean he felt there was something between us? That he wanted there to be something between us? How between us could something be from here to Wisconsin? And what was I supposed to say? Why don't we just skip the next couple of dates and have it off right here on the table? What in the world was I going to do with an out-of-town romance? With a guy I didn't even know before the big move? This wasn't camp. This wasn't a vacation. I couldn't swear undying love and fidelity to someone I'd only be able to see at Christmas and for summers. But, there he was. Smiling sheepishly. Offering me a life-style even I couldn't be stupid enough to want.

On top of that, I didn't even know what this meant for the short term. What were we supposed to talk about now? The stir-fried garlic string beans? Would staying here mean I was making some sort of commitment? And what would happen when dinner was over? Somehow, I couldn't imagine a simple good-night doing the trick.

Contrary to my expectations, though, the rest of the dinner went just fine. The usual conversations about apartments, movies, my ex-husband, his wife and, in honor of his new job offer, cows. And while we talked, I noticed, somewhat uncomfortably, that he was becoming more attractive. The eye contact. The curly hair. The way he leaned forward in his chair when he spoke. His features weren't changing or anything. My relationship to them was. I'd never trusted beautiful women or handsome men. I'd admired them both, but trusted neither.

Attraction was something else again. Attraction was what it was all about. Using who you were to make the most of what you were born with.

Now here I was with Noah Lowell and he was pulling the attraction game on me. He was growing on me. Quickly. It was happening before my eyes. We were getting together. Getting in sync. And once we were together, I'd go crazy about him. And just when I'd decided to avoid other men, he'd move and we'd spend the next fifty years talking about the difficulties of long-distance love.

We got the bill and split the check one more time. He was getting the job, but he hadn't gotten that paycheck yet. We walked. There was no place to go. Noah spoke vaguely about a novel by some banned Russian that I'd probably love, which set us looking for an open bookstore. Then he kissed me.

It wasn't passionate. The kind of kiss that caused others on the street to sneer and smirk. It was more old-fashioned in a way. Like a declaration of intentions: "I'd just like you to know that my feelings for your daughter are honorable, sir."

Of course, not too honorable. Which set me thinking how the evening would end. But there didn't turn out to be all that much to think about. We never found that open bookstore. We did end up at a subway stop. Where he asked me to join him for dinner at his apartment the next night. Date number three and counting. And we kissed one more time. Then he took the uptown train home. And I headed for Brooklyn, counting all the way the reasons why I shouldn't be as happy as I was that things with Noah suddenly looked very good indeed.

THIRTY-TWO

♦

It was five blocks from the subway to my front door. Three of those blocks were on Atlantic Avenue, where stores were open all night and always busy. The other two took me a little more off the beaten track, more trees on the sidewalk and a lot less light, and gave the apartment just enough charm for the landlord to charge a hundred a month more than for the apartments just one block away.

I was still thinking of Noah as I climbed the stoop to my front door, having resolved that the intelligent thing to do would be to put stringent limits on my involvement with

someone destined to live halfway across the country. Even i
we ended up sleeping together, there would have to be
limits. That settled, I put my key in the lock.

"Rita. Where you been?"

It was another late-night welcoming committee. Only thi
one wasn't as much of a surprise. He was standing between
the only streetlight on this side of the street and me, so that
couldn't see anything more than a silhouette, but all those
years of marriage have a way of burning a voice into the
memory banks. The voice was the same, only it was a little
louder than usual, the words a little more slurred.

"What are you doing here, Frank?"

Even in the two steps he took to get closer to me, I could
see his movements were heavy, his outer limbs threatening
to revolt against his brain's control at any moment.

"I just wanted to see you, baby."

I still couldn't see that smile, but I knew it was there a
well as I'd known his voice.

"Yes."

"How're you doing?"

"Fine."

"Can I come in?"

"Why?"

I took the key out of the lock and held it in my hand
Having Frank in my room, drunk, after midnight was no
the most appealing way to end what had turned out to be
something of a pleasant evening. Frank just stood there
Hands in his pockets. Rocking as though it was easier to stay
balanced that way than standing still.

"Come on, Rita. Don't be so cold."

"It's late, Frank. Call me tomorrow."

I tried to figure how long it would take to unlock the
door, get inside, and shut the door behind me. I wondered i

Frank would try to stop me. If he'd break the window in the old oak door to get inside. And if I'd have the nerve to turn him in if he did.

Only Frank's move came too unexpectedly for me to react in time. I'd been waiting for the direct attack. A lunge for my leg. A grab at my hair. But Frank didn't even twitch. He just started crying. First a sniffle. Then some sobs. Maybe I was wrong, maybe this wasn't Frank. But there it was.

"I'm falling apart, Rita."

"I'm sorry."

"I don't know what's happening to me."

I didn't either, but it wasn't fair to dump it on me. Not tonight, anyway.

"You need help, Frank."

"Help me, Rita."

"Fine. Go home. If you still want help when you wake up, give me a call."

I was playing the hardass, but it was getting tough. Hell, I'd been married to the man. There was a time when I'd thought he was the one and only person in the world for me. Now here he was, standing all slumped over, pathetic. A word I'd never thought I'd use to describe him.

"Carla threw me out, Rita. I got no place to go. I got no money. Help me, Rita."

"Frank, I'd like to help. But . . ."

"She thought you and I were getting it on. She knew there'd been others, but she has this thing about you. Then with the drinking and everything. Maybe if you just called her . . ."

So now it involved me. He was playing his part perfectly and he was beginning to wear me down.

"Why would she listen to me?"

"Please, Rita. Please."

The two sobs in the second "please" did me in. I opened the door. Victory one for Frank. Instantly, the sobs stopped. Even the thick, lurching movements seemed to work their way back under control. He was drunk all right. And worse. The smell coming off the guy now that he was close wasn't only the smell of the whiskey he'd been drinking; Frank had liquor in his body odor. He was sweating the stuff. But he just might be a little more in control in this state than I could imagine. Even so, if he was getting things back together, it would only be short-term, a second wind.

I walked up the stairs keeping as much distance as I could from the guy. And I noticed that with every step he took, he refamiliarized himself with the building he used to live in. Here he was, walking up the same old stairs with the same old woman. By the time we got to my front door, Frank was back in his element, everybody's best friend, king of the world.

"All right, Frank. You come in for five minutes. We'll call your wife. I'll give you a cup of coffee. Then you go home. Okay?"

"Whatever you say, Rita. You're saving my life, darling. I won't forget it."

"I wish you would."

I unlocked the door. Before I could even put the water on for coffee, Frank had taken his jacket off and collapsed on the bed. And the funny thing was, it didn't seem that strange. Hell, the bed had been Frank's before he'd even met me. He'd collapsed like that every night after we'd been out. It was like that old "Time Tunnel" TV show. First Wilsey. Now Frank. Everybody was coming back. Rita Noonan, this is your life. Who'd be next? My first-grade teacher, who remembered the cutest pictures I used to draw? And would they all follow Wilsey right on out of my life as well? It was too much.

"Off the bed, Frank."

He pretended not even to realize what he'd done, and acted as embarrassed as he could be that he'd crossed the line as much as he had.

"Oh, sure, sure. I'm sorry. Hey, Rita, you know I appreciate this. I wouldn't . . ."

He looked around.

"How long you been living in this little place?"

"Counting the time with you, eleven years."

"Eleven years. And I was here for three years before that. You ever miss the old times?"

"No."

"Hey, come on, Rita. I mean, I'll admit it. I miss things the way they were. Not all the time. But I miss them."

"How were they, Frank? Those old times."

"What do you mean?"

It probably wasn't the best time to start working the case, but there were some questions I had to ask and he was the one who'd invited himself over.

"Why were you giving money to Wilsey all these years?"

Frank laughed a little too loudly.

"What are you talking about? I told you I hadn't seen the guy."

"You told me a lot of things, Frank. Tell me about who was paying you off. Tell me about Stub Kinnon. Tell me about why Wilsey was blackmailing you."

"You don't know what you're talking about, Rita. There was no blackmail. You've got to believe me, Rita. It's important you believe me."

"Call your wife, Frank."

Suddenly, the tears started welling up again.

"I can't."

"Call her or get out."

"Look at me. I'm falling apart, Rita. Look at me. Let me stay. Just tonight. On the floor. I promise, I'll sleep it off. Shower up. She'll take me back. You got to let me stay, Rita, you got to."

"Get out."

"Rita."

"Get out, Frank, or I'll call the police."

He started walking closer.

"You were never like this before."

I picked up the phone.

"Put down the phone, Rita."

I dialed 911 and waited for an operator to pick up the phone.

"Come on, Rita. Tell me you miss me. For old times' sake."

No operator was picking up. I'd remember this the next time some jerk mayor claimed it was necessary to cut services. Frank was almost on top of me now.

"Stay away from me, you son of a bitch, or I'll kill you."

If I'd meant to scare him away, the effect I got wasn't so desirable. It was as though I'd just said the last thing Frank needed to hear. I was the one last person to get on his case.

"You don't have to talk to me like that."

They still hadn't picked up on the other end. I decided to fake it.

"This is Rita Noonan, 673 DeGraw Street. Please send a patrol car immediately. There's a man in my apartment who's trying to attack me."

"Don't do this to me, Rita."

The pleading in his voice was diminishing. In its place was a growing threat.

"Hurry."

"Rita."

He reached suddenly to grab the phone from my hand, but grabbed my arm instead. I reached with my other hand for a knife on the counter, but Frank grabbed that arm, too.

"You going to kill me, Rita?"

He spread my arms apart and pressed his body close up against me.

"Get off me, Frank."

"You used to like me, baby. Come on, just give it a try. We'll make it this time. I swear."

He leaned his sweating face close and forced a foul-breath kiss on me. He was closing in on a line that couldn't be crossed without repercussions. All right, so he was drunk. He'd screwed up his family life. If things stopped here, I could listen to the excuses and the whole thing could be made to appear less harmful than it was.

But Frank didn't look like he had any intention of stopping here. And I knew from some women's experiences and even from stories Frank told me that things would go a lot easier for me if I could tie Frank to this apartment and showed there was a struggle.

He brought my arms down to my side, pushing me with his body back into the kitchen until he had me up against the wall. He was beginning to thrust into me with his pelvis.

"Come on, baby, just pretend that you love me. I need you so bad."

He was muttering. To himself, really. All I really got was the periodic blasts of his breath in my face. I waited for him to kiss me again, then reached up suddenly and bit him hard in the face. He jerked back, but I held on with my teeth, biting down harder until I could taste his blood in my mouth.

Frank let go of my arms. He put both hands on my face. Squeezing hard. Trying to push me off. But I was already against the wall. And there was no place to push. I reached up with my hands, wishing, as I did so, that I could grow my nails longer than they were, and raked them across his face.

With that, Frank screamed and pulled back. He looked at me, confused, as if he couldn't understand why I didn't want to jump into his arms. I didn't waste a second. I reached for a box of salt on the counter, grabbed a handful and threw it in all those places where I'd just drawn blood.

"You fucking bitch."

He started to reach for me again, but I threw a second handful in his eyes. He rolled away, giving me just enough room to reach the knife he'd prevented me from grabbing earlier.

"Now get the fuck out of here, Frank. Get out before the cops come. Get out before you blow your whole goddamned career."

His eyes were red from the salt. He stared at the knife, wondering if I knew how to use it, remembering he'd been the one who taught me. Wondering if it wouldn't be better if maybe I didn't just go ahead and use it anyway. He kept staring until slowly his eyes went dull.

"I wasn't going to do anything, Rita."

"Sure you weren't."

"Do you want me to leave?"

"Now, Frank."

He stared at me for a minute. The threat was gone. He just didn't want to admit he'd tried to rape me. It was as if he was trying to think of the right line, the right joke that would make everything all right.

That was when the buzzer rang. It was a stupid thing to do. After all, it was after midnight, and there were any number of people out there who wanted to see me roughed up, but I buzzed up without even asking who it was. Odds were, whoever it was would help me out with Frank. And if not, Frank was still here, and he owed me plenty.

If it hadn't been over before, it was over now. Frank looked down at his hands. Just realizing what they'd been doing.

"Rita, I'm . . ."

He moved closer. There was no threat in the move, but I kept my knife steady.

"I . . ."

There was something he wanted to say, but he wasn't going to say it tonight. He turned suddenly, grabbed his coat from the bed, then ran out the door. It was adding insult to injury. Leaving me alone when I didn't even know what was coming to meet me up the stairs.

I held the knife tightly, wishing I'd had a reason to bring the company gun home with me tonight. With one threat gone and another potential one coming up the stairs, it would have been welcome. I didn't relax my grip until I saw Evie Weber turn the corner at the bottom of the stairs.

THIRTY-THREE

♦

She'd arrived like a savior, but there were tears streaking down her face and she was clutching an overnight case with white-knuckled hands that would ache when she finally let go like they probably hadn't hurt since she was a kid and tried to let go of a swing set. She'd done her job well. The last thing it looked like she needed was for me to tell her my troubles.

"Evie. Are you okay?"

It was the standard dumb question. What would she be doing in a stranger's apartment after midnight if she were okay? At least I'd shown I remembered her name. I hoped that was enough to let her know she'd made the right decision in coming here.

"They kept calling."

"Who called you?"

I seemed to be stuck on the standard questions, but right now that seemed a whole lot better than breaking out in hysterics.

"I thought it was my mother. I wasn't going to answer the phone. But it kept ringing. They said they'd kill me if I gave you the book. I told them I didn't know about any book, I haven't seen any book, I don't know anything. Then they told me to remember what happened to Wilsey. And they told me to give them the book or the same thing would happen to me. And they kept calling and calling. They wouldn't talk. They'd just hang up. And keep calling. You wrote your address on your card. I didn't know what else to do."

She was holding the card like a lifeline, showing it to me like I might need proof that I'd given it to her. We stood there a second.

"Are you okay?" she asked.

"I'm fine."

The words were right, only I was still hyperventilating.

"I'm sorry if it's a bad time. Only please don't ask me to leave. I'm so scared."

About the only thing that could have brought me back into control right now was helping someone who was worse off than I was. At least I hoped so. It was only then that I realized my standing there with a kitchen knife in my hands was probably not helping matters much.

I put the knife back in the kitchen.

"You did the right thing, Evie. Come in."

I ran my hand through my hair, trying to put things back

in place as best I could, give Evie a safe place to fall apart. Only this Frank thing just wasn't going away. She was nervous. And I was shaking. And the brandy I poured wasn't doing much of anything.

I tried my best to fake it. We talked for hours. At first about Wilsey. Using the professional thing to keep it together. About what she might be able to tell me about the caller, which mostly amounted to the fact that he was scary. About what I might have gotten her involved in, letting her in on the basics of the case. Under the circumstances, she deserved that.

But with the drinks and the hour, the conversation strayed. We talked about violence. How it affected me, how common it was, how I could live with it. About what being a detective was like. About investigation, of course. But also about the boredom of stakeouts, the constant encounter with desperate spouses, the close working situations with people you'd never in a million years choose as friends.

And then suddenly it started to come. Tears I hadn't cried for years. Heaving sobs. My body racked and shivering. I was so cold.

Evie sat there at first. Some protection I'd turned out to be! Then she wrapped a blanket around me and before I knew it I was telling this stranger all about Frank, about our marriage, about his cheating, about how that made me feel sexually, and how I felt now that I was about to go out with a guy whose wife was some sort of dynamo, and things I hadn't even realized bothered me until now.

"Was that him?"

I nodded.

"What did he try to do to you?"

When I didn't answer, she said, "Do you want to call the police?"

"Nothing happened."

We sat there a moment.

"The hell it didn't."

Evie smiled as warmly as she could, and soon the shakes were gone. By the time I started looking through my closet for the nightgown I'd stopped wearing with Frank's encouragement and an extra one I recalled receiving from someone for some reason, it occurred to me just how long it had been since I'd had anyone to talk to outside of whoever it was I was seeing. The last close woman friend I'd had dated back to junior high. Ever since then I'd either kept to myself or spent time with men. It wasn't a decision I'd made or anything. It just happened. And being married to a cop hadn't helped.

Now here I was handing a nightgown to this scared, cute, chubby woman and inviting her to sleep in my bed with me where we'd probably talk some more, this time about God knows what and I'd probably even giggle. I'd stay up till dawn and confess all my deepest, darkest secrets. We'd promise to have lunch at least once a week and set each other up with all the single men we'd ever met. We'd go shopping, work out together, and give each other makeup tips. The start of a friendship that she'd document in her memoirs fifty years from now. Either that or I'd read in the *Times Book Review* in a month or two that she'd stolen Wilsey's book and blown him away.

THIRTY-FOUR

◆

Evie left for work a half hour before I did. By that time I'd pretty much convinced her that the caller had just been trying to frighten her. People who want to kill these days just do it. No big deal. And they don't spend all day talking to the victim about it. Of course, it was also possible Evie's caller was hopelessly out of touch with the latest trends, but my status as a detective seemed to give credibility to my opinion. That, and the fact that the caller hadn't bothered to follow her.

So Evie left, with explicit instructions to call the cops if anything even the least bit threatening happened and to call me if she just wanted to talk. We'd also agreed to a lunch next week and a possible vacation in the Caribbean some time next winter. After that I put on a pair of fuzzy slippers I hadn't worn in fifteen years, pulled out a box of oatmeal, brewed up a cup of tea and had another, more private, cry about Frank.

I thought about curling up in bed and staying there for the rest of the day, dropping the whole Wilsey thing. No one was paying me. No one was waiting for the results. If I wanted to stay home, there was really no reason not to. Only I'd opened something, I'd chased down leads, let people know they were under suspicion, let people know someone thought they were involved. Even if I wanted to walk away from the whole thing, Frank had shown me it wouldn't be that easy. And now I'd brought Evie into it, too.

So with the greatest of effort, I forced myself out the door, intending to go to the office. I'd tell Malcolm where I was in the case and hope that in the telling one of us would notice something I'd missed. I tried not to think of the groveling I'd have to do to get Malcolm to do that listening. I checked to see if Frank was outside waiting for me before letting go of the door.

"Why didn't you tell me?"

It was Rafe. He was standing across the street. There was a chill in the air and he was wearing an old polyester Windbreaker with the same powder-blue fishing hat. He held his copy of the *Post* under his arm and crossed over to meet me.

"Why didn't you tell me, Rita?"

He walked with a fast, determined stride of his stubby legs. As he got closer, I could see he was stiff, trying to fight off limping. His eyes were red. One was swollen shut. His jaw was tight and quivering. There were visible bruises and somehow I figured I was responsible. One more person ecstatic that I'd come into his life.

"Rafe, my God, what happened?"

"Why didn't you tell me about the new job, Rita?"

"I just found out yesterday. I was going to tell you. I swear."

"Didn't you think I'd want to know? Didn't you think it would affect me?"

"I said I was going to tell you."

He was walking next to me now, but he couldn't bring himself to look my way. It was like he'd practiced this speech the whole way over and then a few more times while he waited for me to come out. He didn't want to get me talking. It might break up his rhythm.

"I've been busting my ass for this company. Following this person and that. Taking pictures that are worse than the ones in the magazines I refuse to read. Turning over the money to you and the fat man. Why do you think I do that, Rita? What do you think I'm thinking?"

Clairvoyance not being my strong suit, I waited for him to continue. It didn't take long.

"I'm thinking I got a late start in this business. I'm thinking I've got to catch up. I've got a lot of learning to do. And you know Malcolm ain't going to help me any. So that leaves you. You and experience." He slammed his copy of the *Post* against his leg. "I've got my eyes open, Rita. Malcolm doesn't like me. He doesn't want me around. Maybe it's me. Maybe it's 'cause I don't wear a skirt. It doesn't matter. He's getting old. He's going to want to get out sooner or later. I kept thinking maybe you and I could make a go of things. I could carry my weight by then."

It was a nice way to start the day, shattering the dreams of someone who'd saved my life. Messing him up just after he'd already taken a beating. We kept walking quietly.

"You know if you leave, the whole thing's over."

"Yeah."

Suddenly, the little guy looked up. "Are we going anywhere?"

I shrugged.

"Anywhere around here we can get a cup of coffee?"

We turned into a doughnut dive where the pastries on the racks looked like they were half-fossilized. The tart behind the counter took one look at Rafe's face and did her best to keep her distance. I ordered a coffee. Rafe got himself a cocoa. With whipped cream. He took a sip, giving himself a kid's mustache.

"What happened, Rafe?"

He raised a hand and touched the bruise on his face as gently as he could.

"I don't really know." He laughed. "I was sitting in the office alone. Malcolm went home early again. Couldn't catch his breath or something. The next thing I know, these three big guys come in and start waling away on me."

"They didn't say anything?"

Rafe took another hit off his cocoa. He wasn't looking at me.

"Not much. They asked if you worked there."

"Oh."

What was there to say. Not only was I walking out on the guy, I'd gotten him beat up as a going-away present.

"Do you know who they were? Did they say anything?"

Rafe just shook his head.

"I'll tell you one thing, though. They were big. Real big. This one guy had a neck like my thigh. Son of a bitch, they were big."

They'd left no calling card, but guys that big traveling in packs have their own way of announcing their presence. Right now, it looked like my leaning on Brotell had just paid off. I resisted sharing the satisfaction I felt in figuring correctly that Brotell was pushing steroids. On the other hand, there wasn't all that much satisfaction to share.

"There won't be an agency for us to run, will there?"

"I don't know."

"All this crap, all this garbage, the late hours, the extra time. . . . Do you know I sometimes follow people on my way home just to see how long I can do it before they notice? Where's it going to get me? I told my wife to just wait, she'd see, things were going to get better. Some better. I'm going to lose the lame job I've got."

He was a friend. And he had a right to lay on the guilt.

"What do you want me to say, Rafe?"

"I want you to say you won't take the job."

"They're talking about eighty thousand, benefits, and a chance for advancement, Rafe."

The little guy drained what was left of his cocoa, wiped off his mustache, and ordered another.

"Then take me with you." He smiled for the first time. "You know, the funny thing was, I was making an effort to cut back on the bitching all the time."

He touched his face again. And winced.

"Just what the hell are you into, Rita?"

We sat there drinking for about an hour while I told him about Wilsey and Frank and Kinnon and Max. I told him about Wilsey and Nell. And Bobby and Rosa Sarmiento. There was the surprise visit from Jesus Rantz. And the threats from just about anyone who'd ever known Wilsey. I also told him about the bodybuilding dentist who pushed steroids.

Rafe just nodded his head slowly.

"I worry about you, Rita. I mean, what if I hadn't been there yesterday? What if it had been you?"

"I guess I would have got the beating."

"Yeah, and I know you've taken beatings before, but, my God, Rita, kid, you can't do this kind of thing. Hell, these guys were serious. I don't even want to think about it."

"Thank you."

"For what? This new job you're getting . . ."

"I didn't get it yet."

"You'll get it. They deal with a better class of people?"

I shrugged.

"I don't know. Maybe it's not such a bad idea."

Which brought us right back to the doughnut shop. We were still sitting across from each other. The problem still hadn't changed. Nothing had changed. Rafe even had another whipped-cream mustache.

"Shit. Take that job. You don't have any choice. Hell, if it was my chance, I'd take it."

"And what will you do?"

He laughed.

"I'll probably hang on to the fat man as long as he tries to make a go of it. Then, when I get sick and tired of him blaming me for the whole thing going down the tubes, I'll walk. Hey, if I'm lucky, I'll have enough experience to hook up somewhere else. One of those big agencies. Like the one that fired me before you guys took me on. Where I'll do a piece of this job and a piece of that one and never know what I'm doing or why but I'll make a little better money and I'll have a little better security and sooner or later I'll retire. And at least I'll have got to do something I always wanted to. Don't worry about me, Rita."

"I should have called you."

"Yeah."

We got up off of our plastic-covered spinning stools and headed into the city. Rafe had been a pain in the ass lately, but he was all right. I couldn't help slipping him a token when we got on the subway. It wasn't much, but he understood.

As we rattled across the river, he looked over to me and shook his head.

"You know, no offense, but I keep thinking, why you? I've been working job after job. I've been doing a good job. And if I leave, you could replace me, no problems. You find a stiff in your apartment, for Christ's sake. Bang. They love you and can't live without you. I tell you, Rita, publicity is everything."

THIRTY-FIVE

◆

Enough was enough. I'd let Max get away with his little code of cop ethic as long as I could. All right, so he didn't want to come forward and name names of who was on the take nine years ago. And maybe there was something to that. If a guy'd stayed clean ever since, maybe sleeping dogs were best left lying. But somewhere out there a dog had woken up. Two people had been killed. Another threatened. I'd almost been raped. And Rafe had just been beaten. The longer I stumbled around in the dark, the more of this nonsense I could expect. I went down to the precinct unannounced to put the screws to Max.

I wasn't naive enough to believe I could get Max to inform on every dirty cop he'd ever known. He'd never do it, even if I threatened to reveal where I got the copies of the police personnel files. He wouldn't even have to bring up any names. I had plenty of names to bring up already. What I wanted was anything he could tell me about those names. I wanted to close this Wilsey thing now.

Max looked up from his desk.

"Oh, Jesus, Rita."

Whatever plausible benign explanations there might be for my coming to visit the guy would be eliminated by anyone looking at Max's reaction to my arrival.

"What are you doing here?" he whispered.

He stood up and grabbed his jacket from the back of his chair.

"We've got to talk."

"Oh, Jesus."

Max took my arm and ushered me out of the precinct station. It wasn't safe here, he said. He didn't want to go to any nearby coffee shops either. Being seen with me right around now was about as desirable as cancer.

"I told you never to come to the precinct, Rita," he said, shaking his head. "I don't know. I just don't know."

We finally settled on a dairy restaurant three blocks from the station. It wasn't far enough away to please Max, but it had the advantage of not serving meat, thereby excluding most veteran cops while not being particularly healthful, which excluded the handful of mavericks not put off by the first restriction.

Max ordered something right away, but he was too nervous to eat it. It was all he could do to absentmindedly stir his cup of coffee.

"Did you hear about Bobby Sarmiento?"

Max was doing his best to put off the inevitable. And as much as I wanted to hurry him along, there was no way I would know what happened unless I'd been there, and that was one hassle I didn't need. I did my best to fake some interest as he ran down the details of the killing as much as he knew.

"The thing of it is, Rita, Sarmiento was Wilsey's partner. They'd been busted together a couple of times."

"I know, Max."

"This whole thing's getting pretty weird. If anyone up top catches on, there won't be any way to kill the investigation. Rita, I'm really worried. Really."

By now, the sour cream had melted all over his potato pancakes, resulting in an unappetizing mess. Max waited till that moment before he finally put a bite in his mouth. He shook his head in despair, then called a waiter over and ordered me a vegetarian chopped liver.

As long as we were stuck on old news, I asked if it was the same gun.

"No. The bullets weren't even the same caliber."

That didn't mean that the same person wasn't behind both hits. Especially if professionals were involved. It just meant there were two guns involved and no one was out there trying to make my job any easier. It was time to find out if Max could.

"Tell me about Stub Kinnon, Max."

Max's fork started working overtime tapping against his plate. Police work was supposed to be a private matter and any time he shared inside information it affected him in a physical kind of way.

"Stub was a good cop."

"I know. Stub was a great cop. Climbing out on bridges to talk down jumpers. Saving stray dogs that get tortured by kids. Busting down doors to take out dealers. The guy was over at my house for dinner every week. We all loved him. We all loved Wilsey. For a while. Tell me about Stub Kinnon."

Max just sat there.

"Max, it will only get worse."

He looked down at his meal as if it were getting farther and farther away from him, and when he spoke, his voice seemed to come from a great distance.

"There were only rumors. Rita, I didn't want to know, so I didn't find out. I think maybe something was going on. I don't know if it was the mob or something less organized. Maybe he was just keeping some of the money he made on a bust. I don't know."

"How about Rantz and Morris?"

"I don't know. We weren't in the same division. I really don't know."

"How about Frank?"

"Frank was clean."

"He was paying money to Wilsey."

"Maybe he felt sorry for the guy."

"Then why did he lie about it? Max, was Wilsey black-mailing Frank?"

"No."

"Then why was he paying?"

"For Stub, okay. For Stub. When Stub died, he'd been paying Wilsey and nobody knew about anything and Frank just wanted to keep it that way. Look, Rita, he'd kill me if I told you. If I told anybody."

I ordered another cup of coffee. We both sat staring into the table.

"What do you think?"

"I'm not working this case, you know."

He picked up a packet of Sweet'n Low and began turning it around and around on the table.

"It could still have been Sarmiento."

"He's dead, Max."

"What does that mean? The guy was into drugs. You know, when we told the wife, she starts crying and carrying on, the usual stuff about losing her man and being alone and the whole thing being our fault and what was she going to do now with five kids. Next thing you know, we find an ounce of raw opium and a bag full of steroids wrapped in her nightgowns."

I smiled, without any feeling behind it. Little Rosa had planned to keep whatever inheritance she'd been able to find.

"The thing of it is, Rita, this is what we've been looking for, isn't it?"

"What do you mean?"

Max had ordered another cup of coffee. The restaurant still had the old-fashioned kind of sugar that came in a glass container and not in the packets. Max poured some into his spoon, then stirred it into his coffee.

"I've got to cut back on the sugar. I had a physical, you know. My sugar's way too high. Eileen's getting worried."

"Max, what the hell are you talking about?"

He hated it when I swore. He sat straight up in his chair, getting rid of his ever-present slump if only for a second. Still nervous, he ran his tongue over his lips, leaving them dry as ever.

"Don't you see, Rita? With Sarmiento gone, the whole thing could go down as a drug thing. Wilsey and his buddy try to muscle their way into an operation. They put the bite on one of the big boys and the big boys bit back. It makes sense. We track it down as far as we can. If it falls apart, it falls apart. If it doesn't, no one has to go digging where they don't belong."

It was the hard sell, or Max's version of it anyway. Wilsey was dead. He posed a threat. Now there was a convenient way to sweep the body under the carpet. If only I'd go along.

"Drugs?"

"Wilsey was involved. We know that. Those guys are always killing each other. We hardly ever catch them. It's one of those closed cases even if we don't catch the guy."

"And my apartment?"

Max went back to stirring his coffee.

"If the hit was drug-related, and it went down at my place, what does that say about me?"

His eyes were focused on the little swirls and eddies following the glide of his spoon through the now-cooling liquid.

"How am I supposed to keep the business together, Max? Come on down to Ortner and Lloyd Investigations. If we can't solve your problem, we can sell you something to kill the pain. Jesus, Max, you're asking too much."

"Rita, this is my career. It's my life. It's a lot of people's lives."

"And it's my life, too."

The last lines had gotten a little loud even amid the clatter of dishes from the waiters running back and forth and the chatter from the older merchants sitting around us. Naturally, their noise died away as ours rose, leaving everyone to stare at us.

Max didn't say a word. As far as I was concerned, that improved the conversation immensely. But sitting there in silence, I started getting this obnoxious thought. What would be so bad about writing the case off? What would be so bad about pulling out? Sure, I'd opened some doors. I'd even gotten a couple of people involved who'd just as soon never have met anyone who even looked like me or Wilsey. But that would wash out if I dropped the case, if I left the agency, if I went the corporate route. It would all be so easy.

I don't know how long we'd been sitting there when a sick look began to cross Max's face. Assuming it wasn't the pancakes, I turned to see the cause of the look.

Walking into the restaurant were Jesus Rantz and Lenny Morris. They must have known we were here because they didn't even make a pretense of looking around. They walked straight over to our table and pulled up some chairs.

"Hey, sweetheart. Max here telling you the news about the Sarmiento kid? Oh, it was pretty. One shot. Right here."

Rantz put his index finger squarely in the center of my forehead, making sure to hold his cigarette over my lunch in the process.

"How long you been here?" Max asked.

"Lenny and I didn't show up till a good half hour after the fact and, man, I'm telling you, the brains, the skull, they were all right where you'd want them. Only this little tiny hole and a small puddle of blood and cranial fluid. A little Bounty and some Top Job would clean the whole thing right up."

"How long you been here?" Max hated it when people made him look bad. Especially on the job. No matter how often it happened, he never got used to it.

"Long enough, dickhead. Come on, let's take a walk."

"I'm not going with you, Rantz."

"Buddy, if you haven't scored with the bitch by now, a couple of more minutes ain't going to make a difference. Why don't you do the right thing and let Lenny take a shot at her?"

Max was getting red. He'd never learned the ability to bullshit, especially when sex came into the picture. He'd probably gotten excuses from his doctor and missed out on the gym locker-room thing altogether. I wasn't exactly thrilled with the way Rantz went on about things myself, but getting pissed would only get me more of the same. Besides, Max was handling that side of things well enough for both of us right now.

"Max, I'd like to talk to the lady for a minute if you don't mind."

Lenny was speaking more quietly than usual. For some reason the color ebbed from Max's face and the big man lumbered off away from the table with his tormentor. Lenny looked at the table, then at me.

"You like this food?"

"It's okay."

Lenny shook his head.

"Jesus been giving you a hard time?"

A list of Rantz's offenses would only seem petty. I figured a shrug would get Lenny's imagination working, which could only work to my benefit.

"What have you got on Wilsey?"

It was remarkable how well the whole good-cop—bad-cop thing worked. Here he was, speaking civilly to me, and I was ready to tell him everything I'd learned about Wilsey, Sarmiento, or anybody else for that matter. Hell, I'd confess to the killings myself if I thought it would cheer Lenny up.

"He was mixed up in all the usual things you could get mixed up in. Any one of them could have gotten him killed."

Lenny nodded slowly. His words, carefully chosen, followed along at the same pace.

"I want to apologize for Jesus. He's a territorial kind of guy and when someone he cares about gets threatened, he tends to go on the attack."

This time, it was my turn to nod. If Lenny Morris had a confession to make, the last thing I wanted to do was say something that would change his mind.

"Some years back, when Wilsey was on the force, some of us got involved in some things we shouldn't have. It wasn't big-time. We weren't shaking anyone down. We weren't turning our heads and letting things slide. And we weren't pocketing what we were busting people for selling. At least, most of us weren't."

Lenny took out his handkerchief and mopped away at the mini-Niagara that had begun to flow down his oversized forehead. He was beginning to remind me of this fat kid in elementary school who always seemed to be sitting in the principal's office as I walked by. It never looked like a comfortable position to be in.

"What we were doing was not turning in all the cash we'd confiscate. Some guys kept watches and jewelry, but mostly it was cash. We tried to look out for each other, keep things from getting out of hand. If it wasn't for Jesus . . ."

"Rantz wasn't involved?"

"Jesus took me away fishing for a weekend and beat my ass like it'd never been beaten before. He broke up the group I was hanging with. Then he did what he could to bury the whole thing. I've been clean ever since. I want to bury Wilsey. I want to bury him real bad. What will it take?"

"Were you paying him off?"

"I was giving him some bucks. More informally, really. No fixed times or amounts. Just here and there. Lately, he'd been wanting more. I can't say I'm sorry he's gone."

"But you didn't do him?"

"I told you I've been clean."

"Why are you telling me this?"

Lenny shrugged. "It's gone too far, I guess. There've been some calls. Some other stuff. I just don't want Jesus to go down for me."

I must have hesitated a little in responding. Lenny took it as some sort of sign.

"Well, I said what I had to say. You think about it. I know what this thing means to you. It wasn't fair to put the pressure on. There won't be any more."

He pushed back his chair and slid his gut sideways so he could get out from under the table. He started slowly for the exit.

Lenny left and a few minutes later Max returned. This time he had his wallet out. I anticipated his picking up the tab. Instead, he inundated me with pictures of his new wife and her kids. It was his last pitch and he was giving it everything he could.

"They seem like nice people."

"They're the greatest," he affirmed glumly.

And that was that. We finished up in silence, until we were just about to leave.

"Frank told me not to tell you this, but I think you should know. He took a leave from work. He seemed in really bad shape. He's checking himself into a dry-out clinic."

I wasn't sure how that was supposed to make me feel. Right now the only thing that came to mind was anger. I mean, I was glad he was getting help and everything, but did that make everything okay? Don't worry that I tried to rape you, babe, that was just the alcohol. See? I'm getting help. Isn't that what you wanted? I'll clean myself up and everything will be back to normal. Sure.

THIRTY-SIX

♦

Between what Max and Lenny had told me, there was a lot to rethink. In the last week Frank had gone from being some stoic ivory-tower-type guy to a bribe-paying rapist and now was heading, the rape attempt excepted, toward some sort of heroism of loyalty. Rantz, who'd been one of my favorites for the gun-to-the-head routine, was now a white knight rescuing his fellow officers from their own transgressions. Morris was now this repentant sinner who'd effectively put his life in my hands. And Max, of course, was still Max.

On the other hand, they could have all been lying, and I could catch a bullet in the head on the way home tonight. I decided to swing by the office and check things out with the head man. Everything seemed to be pushing back toward the drug thing, maybe Brotell, maybe the opium boys. And the number Brotell did on Rafe didn't help his cause. Brotell was a bust just waiting to happen, only I wanted to check it out with Malcolm first.

The note from Rafe that was lying on my desk was short and to the point: "Emergency. Meet me at St. Vincent's Hospital A.S.A.P. Malcolm."

There was no elaboration. No indication of what the problem was or how severe things were. I only stopped to lock the door before I was on my way.

I tried to remember what Malcolm looked like the last time I'd seen him. Okay, he'd seemed tired and pale. He'd been tired and pale every day this week.

I should have said something. But what was I going to say? Stop eating all that garbage? Stop sleeping with that woman before she kills you? That wasn't the kind of subject matter I wanted to open up with him. Maybe, if I'd just said something. But what could I have said? You're too old to be messing around like this? You're too old to live out your dreams? A nice thing to say when I'd just told the guy I was halfway out the door to another job already. Why hadn't I stopped by a little more? Why had I let myself get caught up in that fight? Whatever I should or shouldn't have done, it was all my fault.

The cab dropped me off at the main entrance to St. Vincent's. The same building Malcolm came to for his heart attack six months ago. The same place where I'd visited him day in and day out, bringing his mail, learning the more administrative side of the business, listening to him gossip about which nurses were doing what to whom and how he'd tried to get them to do something else to him.

The woman at Information told me where to find Malcolm. Rafe was waiting outside of Intensive Care when I got there. He had his copy of the *Post*, but he was just holding on to it, folding it, unfolding it, staring at a headline without reading it, then folding it again. There were already two or three empty coffee cups on the table next to him.

"I got back from this motel gig. Malcolm wasn't there.

Neither were you. I was just hanging out when I got this phone call. It was a woman. He was in this hotel room. He'd collapsed. When emergency got there, he was alone."

"Is it his heart?"

"They think so. They're hoping it might just be exhaustion, but it looks like the heart again. It was like a dream. I had this video, and I mean, this wife was something to see. I figured, you know how Malcolm gets a kick out of this sort of thing. Jesus."

"Is he going to be okay?"

Rafe just shrugged.

"It's all my fault."

I laughed and Rafe looked over at me.

"It's just that I was thinking the same thing."

"The whole way back to the office today, I'm thinking what a son of a bitch the guy is. I'm thinking I'm finally going to stand up to the guy. I'll give him the video, get him all worked up, then hit him up for a raise, lower hours, and see if we can get him to cough up for a couple of freelancers to pick up the slack. I was cursing the guy out the whole subway ride. I was even talking out loud. Nobody wanted to sit next to me."

It was really bugging the guy and nothing I could say would change that.

"You can't give someone a heart attack by calling them a son of a bitch to yourself on a subway, Rafe," I offered, glad that I hadn't thought anything too nasty about Malcolm myself today.

Rafe just sat there, folding and unfolding his newspaper, knowing in his heart he was responsible for the old man's condition.

We waited for another hour before Malcolm's doctor, a brusque, overweight, frizzy-haired woman, arrived to talk to us. We got through the preliminaries without too much difficulty. Malcolm had had a second heart attack. He was sleeping now.

I could see Rafe looking up to the ceiling and offering a little thanks that he was all right so far. Dr. Reinhaller didn't wait even a moment.

"You work for the patient?"

Her voice was clipped, almost as though she practiced eliminating any trace of compassion from it.

"*With* him. He's my partner."

She looked me up and down, jotted something on her clipboard, then continued.

"He's a private investigator?"

"That's right."

She looked at me again, this time without writing anything.

"Has he been working hard lately?"

I explained how Malcolm had withdrawn from the field-work of the operation and pretty much restricted himself to advisory and administrative duties as well as acquiring new business. I tried to make it seem as though that was a light load. If she'd ever seen him performing those duties, she'd be amazed at how light they could be. Nevertheless, she gave me a glance to let me know what a slime she thought I was to heap that much work on a man still recovering from heart disease.

"Has he been under any stress lately?"

What was I supposed to tell her? That the old fart had been banging his brains out with this killer bimbo? I tried to think of a clinical way to describe the situation, then figured it was better to let Malcolm handle this one on his own.

"Not that I know of."

She then turned to an even more disagreeable topic, asking about the patient's family. Did he have a wife? No. What other family was close? I mentioned the names of the crowd who showed up the last time Malcolm got sick, but, no, there was no one particularly close. By the time I got through with the ice queen's list of questions, I'd gotten so depressed I wondered if it wouldn't be better if she just pulled the plug and got done with the whole thing once and for all. And not just for Malcolm. How many years would it be before I'd be lying inside Intensive Care myself, a couple of employees with mixed feelings about my recovery hanging around outside trying to convince some doctor that my life wasn't quite as pathetic as it sounded?

Dr. Reinhaller must have noticed the effect she had on me. She smiled professionally and set out to finish the job.

"Were you with him when it happened?"

"No. I was in the field."

She looked at me just long enough to make sure I knew she didn't believe me.

"There are signs that the patient had just engaged in some rather strenuous exercise. Also signs that he'd engaged in very recent sexual activity. Yet he was alone when the paramedics found him." She gave me the dirtiest look she had in her repertoire. "If the patient recovers, I will tell him in the future to select more responsible partners."

Satisfied that she'd done the job she'd set out to do, she put her clipboard under her arm, thanked me for my help, flashed the smile they taught her in her course on bedside manner, and bolted as fast as she could.

I tried to manage a smile for Rafe's sake. He was still working on his involvement in Malcolm's being stricken. I couldn't resist taking hold of Rafe's hand.

"He's going to be okay."

And Rafe seemed to agree.

We waited around for a couple of hours before anyone would let us into Malcolm's room. It had all the usual warmth I expected from hospital rooms. Without the flowers. Malcolm was lying there like the proverbial beached beluga. Tubes ran into each of his nostrils. He was breathing a little unsteadily, like he'd been drugged, which he probably had been.

We watched him breathe for about ten minutes.

"I think I'd better get going."

I nodded.

"If he wakes up while you're here, let him know . . . you know."

Rafe turned back and watched Malcolm for another minute or so, then left. I waited another hour before Malcolm opened his eyes. It was only for a moment or two. I wasn't even sure he could see me. But I was there. And Malcolm almost smiled. And I waited another half hour to see if he'd open them again before I finally gave up and left.

THIRTY-SEVEN

♦

I stretched out my legs against Noah's white cotton sheets. The bed was only a full-size, not even a queen. There was barely room to move, he being so tall and everything. It wasn't the kind of bed a man intent on living the wild life would invest in. Not the kind of bed that made it easy to sleep when I was still feeling all the first-time feelings anyway. Noah was still asleep. Easy for him. It was his bed, his apartment, and he wasn't getting paid by my husband to spy on me.

I'd been awake for a few minutes, but I wasn't quite ready to move yet. It was nice lying there. Sometime during the night Noah must have put his arm around me. The fit was good. At the same time, moving might wake Noah, and I wasn't ready for that yet. That meant lying there. And looking around.

Noah's apartment was small. And old. A rare combination. Most studios in the city were renovated some time during the last twenty or thirty years. The slums of the past were mostly human-sized apartments that were unlivable because too many people tried to squeeze into them. The modern strategy was to carve the spaces up like they do old movie theaters, slap on a coat of paint, and install some new fixtures in an attempt to convince potential tenants that someone outside of a prison warden would design life in one room. Even my little cubby had a reasonably new kitchen.

But Noah's room was old. It must have been in the vanguard of the compartmentalization that eventually swept the city. The decor was sparse, a testament either to his temporary status at the university or his having left most of his possessions at home with his wife. There was the bed, of course. Deep green wool blankets. No bedspread. A small oak table with two mismatching chairs that appeared to have been found on the street sat in front of the only window. The view went no further than the building across the air shaft.

Since he was a professor, there was a desk. Also in oak. Also not matching. A laptop computer sat on top. A boom box with a pile of cassettes sat next to it. Boxes of books were stacked around the room. I was tempted to get up and look through them. Book-browsing was one of my secret passions. The relationship could only go so far if I found he had a bookshelf full of *Winning Through Intimidation* or Carlos Castaneda. I resisted the impulse. There was no reason to destroy my illusions just yet.

The only wall decorations were a poster from some exhibit of Robert Frank photographs at the Whitney, an over-sized Italian poster for *The Good, the Bad, and the Ugly*, and a framed photograph and certificate documenting his successful completion of the New York City Marathon. The apartment was neither neat nor sloppy, just cluttered enough to show someone lived here.

Noah moved, lifting his arm, freeing me. I was tempted to bolt. Not just from the bed, but from the apartment and Noah's life. It wasn't embarrassment at having pushed the relationship further than I'd planned sooner than I'd planned. It wasn't that I'd gotten involved with someone who wasn't as terrific as I'd wanted him to be either. It was worse. It had to do with the sex.

In my whole life, first-time sex had been this good only once before. There was always that nerve stuff. He would look forward to it too much. We would both want to get it out of the way. It was more of a relationship landmark than a moment on its own. Except once before. With this cop who'd shown up to investigate an attempted break-in. Then stayed in touch. Wined and dined me, taking me to Umberto's in Little Italy.

Frank was confident. Enough to let me relax anyway. But there was none of that stud thing, like sex was a contest, a performance in which he was competing for top honors. He'd included me. Like we were creating sex together, making it different than it had been for anyone else because it was the two of us who were doing it. And the promise of that first encounter had carried into the rest of our sex life. Unfortunately, Frank also brought that same ability to his sex life with everybody else. And that was that.

Now there was Noah. And I'd figured we'd eventually get down to business. We were getting together. It was even something of a sure thing. If we got along, if this turned into the affair of the century, well, then, great. If not, the guy

was on his way to Wisconsin, giving us each the opportunity
to withdraw gracefully. Only I hadn't anticipated this. I
hadn't anticipated waking in this apartment caught in a time
warp and finding myself in the same bed I'd woken up in
some fifteen years ago. I hadn't anticipated the shaking and
the stirring. I hadn't anticipated saying, "Wow."

What was this supposed to mean? Was this now not a
normal relationship? Something that would grow and develop one way or another in its own direction and at its own
pace? It had all changed. Now I was lying here thinking I'd
probably end up having to marry the guy. We'd be terrifi-
cally happy, or I'd think we were until I'd catch him cheating with someone. We'd get a divorce. He'd become an
alcoholic. Next thing I'd know, he'd be coming back from
Wisconsin and attacking me in my apartment. It was all too
much to consider.

I hadn't come with the intention of sleeping with Noah. It
had crossed my mind. More than that, maybe. But there was
no intention. At least not for last night. There was still
Wisconsin and I wasn't getting any younger. Getting involved in a dead-end relationship now was significant. It
was a choice about my future. Probably a decisive one.
Married or not, I'd probably stay with the business, but if
things didn't work out soon, I'd be a career woman, and
that was something else altogether. If I was lucky, I'd turn
out to be some grand old lady in the field invited to speak
on the role of women investigators at some P.I. association
luncheon. If not, I'd still be locking up the same old door at
the end of another dreary day and wondering what had ever
attracted me to investigating in the first place. Neither alternative had me dancing on the tabletop and, no, I was in no
hurry to tango with Noah Lowell either.

Which meant I'd go to his apartment, eat dinner, and
maybe mess around just enough to be polite before excusing

myself and going home. I could use the excuse that my boss was in the hospital, being careful not to tell him who my boss was or what he did. It wouldn't hurt, either, that I'd arrived late. No matter what the excuse, lateness was always a slap in the face and would help put him out of the mood. Only he'd opened the door glad to see me and truly worried that some dire fate had befallen me. He hadn't asked for an explanation other than my telling him it had been a wild day. He just poured me a beer and let it go.

That was when I'd first started wavering. For the first time in years I felt like I belonged someplace, as if the apartment that now seemed so strange was a shelter, and maybe if I could just find a way to stay here, I wouldn't have to see another body, another widow, another drunk for a long, long time. Even Wisconsin didn't quite seem as bad as it once had. Hell, it might even be a blessing. How would I be able to keep a normal relationship going? "Gee, honey, I'd love to go to the theater with you tonight, but I've got to get some video of the pastor's wife banging the bartender. Maybe some other time."

I'd gotten so used to the job, the demands and the hours, that it always stood me up short when I'd take up with someone who'd balk. There was no nine-to-five. There were no weekends. Everything depended. And the world was ugly. It was not the atmosphere most conducive to the development of a relationship. Malcolm's marriage had gone down. Rafe's was rocky. Maybe relationships just weren't possible. But Wisconsin could be the perfect antidote. He'd be away, so he'd avoid the day in, day out. And maybe I was fooling myself, but when he was around, I could clear my schedule to make time for him.

That left Hannah's legacy and the intimidation factor surrounding it as the sole impediment to the advancement of further involvement. I'd just about decided to take my chances with that when the kiss of death arrived. Noah mentioned his wife. It wasn't the first time he'd done it. And by now I'd gotten used to the fact that most of the men I'd see would have some sort of excess baggage. But there were times to bring up the little woman, and spending your first night with me wasn't one of them.

I put romance on hold and listened while Noah spoke about growing up on Long Island, hanging out with the whole hip intellectual crowd and lusting after this girl he'd grown up lusting after ever since he first met her at temple. It was one of the great unrequited loves that unfortunately somewhere along the line got requited and the next thing he knew he was spending the summer of his sophomore year on the southern coast of Spain as a wedding present from his newly acquired father-in-law.

It was a dream come true. If he took care of his education, she'd take care of their living. He could stay in school as long as he needed to get his degree and live in an apartment appropriate to a girl of Hannah's upbringing. Only no one expected him to end up studying what he'd ended up studying or taking as long as he did to study it. It was like one of those horror movies where a girl watches aghast as her boyfriend is transformed into a giant bug. There was going to be no end to this education. He'd be no lawyer, doctor, or whatever with all the trappings that went with it. He'd be a professor. A film professor, for God's sake. In some shitass little town. And just when she'd finally been able to accept that, he got his degree and found out just how difficult it would be to become a professor, even in those shitass little towns. All she had to show for her marriage was a collection of articles and a guy with a word processor and three part-time jobs who could never hope to afford the house she'd always wanted to live in.

Still, he'd tried to keep things together until she'd started getting jealous. She accused him of bedding down students at each of his jobs. She'd stop by unannounced trying to catch him in his supposed infidelities. She'd even gone so far—imagine it—as to hire private detectives to follow him around. And that's when he'd moved out.

It was the same old story, more or less. Noah'd played it for laughs and there were certainly no tears in the telling of it. I figured he'd told it so I'd know what I was getting into. He was still a married man. The marriage was over. This was what it had been. The divorce was in the works. It was a talk that would have been necessary sometime. It spoke well of the guy that we'd had it early on.

Only the talk should have killed the evening. It would have, too, if I hadn't taken matters into my own hands and kissed the guy. This whole thing was my fault. Next thing I knew I was waking up in this strange bed with this naked man wrapped around me, having spent the night doing God knows what. I had to get out now, run while I still could.

It was too late. Noah opened his eyes. He kissed me. Like it or not, I was going to have to hang around and have breakfast.

THIRTY-EIGHT

◆

Back in high school we'd talked about the glow a girl had the day after having sex. Your basic neon sign announcing her most private affairs to the world. Of course, back in high school her boyfriend had probably taken care of announcing that little detail already. And no matter how many hours I'd spent in front of mirrors since then convincing myself that there was absolutely no basis to the theory, I was still walking carefully when I showed up at the office. It wasn't so much that I was afraid Rafe would find out I had had sex. Wearing the same clothes I wore yesterday would give him a big hint in that direction. Besides, having him think I never had sex wouldn't be all that great either. But having him find out who it was I had sex with would be an absolute disaster. I did a little deep breathing before opening the door and walking inside.

Rafe was sitting in a chair by the window. He'd been staring at the sweatshop across the air shaft.

"I tried to call you. You weren't home. I left a message."

"What?"

"Malcolm's dead."

"What?"

"They called the office first thing this morning. They said he had another attack. Something about some arteries. A blockage. They were right on top of it. He just didn't pull through."

I put my coffee down on my desk and sank into my chair.

"Are you sure?"

It was one of those great questions. What was Rafe going to say? Maybe they were talking about Malcolm's leftist leanings? Maybe they'd called to say he was red, not dead? Still, it was something to say. Rafe just nodded.

"But he looked fine when I left. He was breathing okay. He even opened his eyes a little. If I had known, Rafe, I wouldn't have left. I swear."

"I know."

I sat in my chair and watched the office change in front of my eyes. I looked at Malcolm's desk and Malcolm's chair and thought about Malcolm's name on the door. There'd be no more Danish crumbs in the paperwork. There'd be no one around to push the reclining capacity of that chair to its limits. It wasn't that he'd retired. I'd been hoping that would come about. Malcolm was dead.

I remembered walking into the office seven years ago to ask about signing on as an operative. He was a friend of a friend of a friend and, even at that remove, I was warned he'd try to come on to me. He wasn't what I'd expected. The low-rent office I could deal with. The overweight, sloppy, disheveled person was what caused me trouble. Just not enough Bogart in the guy for my taste. Either for a detective or the stud he fancied himself.

He didn't try to come on to me till my third late night working here. We were on a stakeout. Marital, of course. Malcolm was showing me how to observe, how to take notes, how to take care of bodily functions without leaving the scene of the surveillance. He must have known there'd be action that night. He had the camera ready with the telescopic lens. He had me looking through it, snapping pictures, and describing in detail to him what it was I was seeing.

Nothing happened right then. It was later. In a bar. Over a couple of drinks. When we were going over the notes. Malcolm reached over and took my hand while at the same time rubbing his foot against my calf under the table. That night was also the first time I'd told him no.

There'd been so many running arguments over the years. About sex. About money. About power, initiative, and independence. And since the partnership, it had gotten worse. There was only so much longer I'd be able to work with the guy. Even without Mencia. But I'd always figured he'd be around. Ignoring more doctors. Sneaking more food. Having more attacks. Taking more pills. But living.

"I was on a date last night, Rafe."

There was no reason to bring the guy in on my personal

life. It just seemed so strange to put together last night for me with last night for Malcolm.

"Do you think it would have made a difference if you were sitting in church praying?"

"Maybe."

"And maybe not. You didn't know. You couldn't have. He wasn't well. And he didn't take care of himself."

"Yeah."

We sat there for a while, both of us staring at the empty chair that would normally be straining under its load by now. I finally opened my cold coffee and began to drink.

"What are you going to do?"

"About what?"

"About that job thing."

It wasn't the most appropriate time to bring it up. Malcolm wasn't even buried yet. But if my decision would have had a major impact on Rafe before this happened, now it would be critical. If I left, there would be no more agency.

On the other hand, how could I stay? Malcolm had been right. He was still responsible for bringing in most of our business. Giving Rafe a promotion wouldn't help that. And whether or not I'd been made a partner, it was still his agency. It was his name on the door. And dead or not, I wasn't ready to replace his with mine. So it would go, the guy would die. By the end of the week all traces of his life's work would vanish from the face of the earth.

I took another hit of the coffee and realized for the first time that maybe it wasn't all my decision. I'd just assumed the agency would be mine once Malcolm had gone. It was only the two of us running the show. When he left, it would be mine. But this was a partnership. He had a stake in this thing and that stake could be passed on. What if he hadn't left it to me? What if he'd given it to some nephew or cousin or aunt or girlfriend. A shiver ran down my spine as I thought of Hannah Lowell walking through the door: "Hello, partner."

I shut my eyes. Malcolm had been more than a friend. He'd been part of my life, part of the way I lived. I'd taken seven years to get used to working with him. In some ways that had been harder than learning the job. Now that skill was suddenly useless.

Rafe looked up. "Are you okay?"

"I've got to get out of here. Can you handle things for a while?"

Rafe nodded and I took off.

THIRTY-NINE

♦

I'd had no idea where I was going when I left the office. I just had to get out. Rafe with his questions. The whole claustrophobic office. Not to mention whatever preparations we'd have to make. I wasn't ready to deal with any of it and I didn't want to be there.

Once I'd hit the road, though, I began to realize I wasn't entirely without a plan. Step-by-step, I was getting closer to Rosa Sarmiento's. It was something Max had said. About the drugs. She hadn't thrown them out. She hadn't returned them to their rightful owner. The trick was, did she know who the rightful owner was?

Rosa Sarmiento was wearing black when she opened the door. So was the little girl behind her and two other kids I hadn't seen the first time I came over.

"What you doing here?"

"I want to know who killed Bobby, Rosa."

"I don't know."

"Who killed Bobby?"

"You. You give him crazy ideas. You make him think he's some sort of . . ." She couldn't think of the English word, but her gesture gave the impression of "big shot."

"But I didn't shoot him, Rosa."

Rosa didn't say anything.

"Who did, Rosa?"

Again nothing.

"Was it drugs, Rosa?"

Rosa turned to the girl.

"*Vete.*"

The girl silently left the room, taking the two little ones with her.

"Who was Bobby dealing for?"

If she'd sent the kids out of the room so they wouldn't hear her talk, she still didn't seem too eager to open up.

"Where did the drugs come from, Rosa? The police know he was dealing. They know Wilsey was dealing. They were probably in it together. They think whoever it was they were working for killed them. They shot them both, Rosa. In the head. Maybe it was for Bobby's big ideas. Maybe I gave them to him and maybe he had them way before I ever saw him, but, Rosa, somebody killed your husband. Do you want them to get away?"

Her hand began fingering an imaginary rosary. She brushed some hair away from her face. I was in the right mood to turn up the pressure.

"The police already took the drugs he left here. You can't sell them anymore. There is no money. What are you going to do when they come looking to get the drugs back? Do you really think they'll take you on to work for them if you can't even hold on to one package? They're going to want it back, Rosa."

It was probably more English than the woman could assimilate all at once, but if I slowed up, I'd lose her.

"I'll tell you what I know, Rosa. They were both working for a dentist. Selling steroids. And there was someone else. Selling opium out of Wilsey's apartment building. One of those people killed Bobby. Now who was it, Rosa?"

I'd gone out on a limb, eliminating cops from the Sarmiento killing. I was betting Bobby would never have the nerve or inclination to try to push cops around. Wilsey maybe, but not Bobby. Drugs would be a world where he was more at home, and a guy like Brotell must have looked ripe to be taken down.

"Who was it, Rosa?"

Rosa was going to talk. Whether she knew who it was or not. She had two choices, the steroids or the opium. Who had Bobby tried to threaten in order to get a better deal? Which was more likely to have responded with violence? And more important, which of the two threatened a worse revenge on anyone who identified them?

"Dentist."

I'd known it before she'd even opened her mouth, whether it was true or not. The mighty mite was just not as scary as those Vietnamese characters I'd seen hanging around outside Wilsey's building.

"That's not enough, Rosa. I need a name. From you. I need a name."

"Brotell. He kill my Bobby."

That would be enough to get the police to pay the guy a visit, maybe even with warrants. I wanted to give them more.

"Did you ever see them together, Rosa? Your husband or Wilsey with Brotell. Did you ever see them getting the drugs?"

Rosa thought about it before she decided to commit herself and lie.

"Yes."

Her story would never stand up in court, of course. And they might never prove anything about the murders. But it would give the cops all they'd need to check Brotell out backward and forward, disrupt the guy's business, and send him running for cover.

I was almost tempted to head over there myself. Hand-deliver the message. Let him know just who it was that had nailed his butt.

Instead, I went outside, dropped a quarter in a phone, and dialed Lenny Morris's extension.

"It's Sarmiento's widow. She's willing to testify her husband was pushing steroids for a dentist named Brotell. She thinks Wilsey was, too. She says she saw them in action. And you already found the drugs. She doesn't know if he did the murders, but she knows her husband was trying to shake the guy down."

"What do you think, Rita?"

I'd done my best to wrap the whole thing up in a bow and bring it to a close. What did I think? Did I think Brotell killed anyone? No. Why wouldn't he have killed Rafe? My money was on the opium dealers. At least as far as Sarmiento went. But they were gone now. I didn't know who they were. And they hadn't beat up Rafe.

"I think there's enough truth here for you to at least bust him on the drug thing. And who knows, you might even get lucky with the rest. It's one ending."

I could hear Morris breathing over the phone. Thinking it over. He couldn't be sure how straight I was being with him, but on the other hand he hadn't exactly been straight with me either. And, of course, he could talk to Rosa Sarmiento himself before he did anything. He must have been thinking along the same lines.

"She'll talk to me?"

"That's what she told me."

There was another pause. Pretty soon I'd have to deposit another quarter. Finally, Morris responded.

"Thanks."

I smiled all the way back to the office trying to imagine Brotell's face when the New York Police Department came bouncing into his office to bust him for dealing in front of all his albino clientele. Teach him to mess with my friends.

FORTY

♦

"You fucking bitch."

They were sitting in the office with Rafe. Rafe was in Malcolm's chair, Noah in mine, and Hannah was in the guest chair. Rafe was doing his best to keep things together.

"These are the Lowells. They wanted to see you for a minute."

"We've met."

"I can't believe she told me the truth. I can't believe you work here, Rita."

He'd dressed a little since I left him this morning. Tweed jacket and gray slacks replaced the sweatpants and T-shirt he'd been wearing. He'd covered his bare feet with running shoes. The hair was still pretty wild.

"Noah, I can explain."

It was something to say. I wasn't sure I could back it up.

"You fucking bitch."

Hannah's eyes were swollen and red. Her cheeks looked dirty from whatever makeup had run down onto them. The woman had already had a rough day from Malcolm pulling a Rockefeller on her the night before. Finding out about Noah and me must have been no treat at all. She held tightly to the armrests, less for support than to restrain herself from taking those inch-and-a-half-long nails to my eyes.

"I sure could go for a cup of coffee. Can I get anybody anything?"

It was a great idea on Rafe's part. I wish I'd thought of it.

"I just called Hannah to tell her about the Wisconsin job. I also wanted to tell her I'd met somebody. I wanted to tell her about us. You're the detective. Figure out how I felt when she recognized your name. Then figure how I felt when I found out how she knew you. I can't believe you didn't tell me."

"I paid you to find out who my husband was sleeping with, not to jump in the sack with him yourself. I want my money back."

"Are you sure no one wants any coffee?"

Rafe was shifting in his chair, wanting to get out of the room but feeling too loyal to leave me alone. Noah stood up and stared out the window. There wasn't much to see. Only the sweatshop. He didn't seem to notice.

"I mean, I just keep thinking about it. You're a detective. You're trying to find out if I'm sleeping with someone. What were you? A test case? How much did my wife pay you to do that?"

It was a cheap shot. He was entitled to it.

"She took me off the case."

"Don't call me she. I'm right here. I'm the wife. You're the she."

"When? When were you taken off the case?"

"A while ago. I don't remember exactly. It's been a long week."

"Yeah."

This wasn't going anywhere. The same thing must have been going through Noah's mind. He turned to look at me.

"I just can't believe you lied. You should have said something."

Then he left. Hannah wasn't going to be far behind. It was probably a plan on her part to make me think they were leaving together. From what Noah'd told me about her and from what I'd seen for myself, the one thing I didn't have to worry about was that I'd somehow drive him back into her arms.

She stood up with as much dignity as she could muster. She'd gotten what she wanted, someone to hate, someone to blame for the failure of her marriage, and someday she'd probably even forget how the timing of things meant the marriage was already shot before Noah met me. She crossed the room on her short little legs until she was staring in my face. She could have done just about anything. My bet was a slap. And for whatever reason, I'd pretty much decided to give her at least one shot free and clear.

She put her face no farther than an inch away and stared into my eyes. I waited for the slap for at least half a minute.

"You will never sleep with my husband again, slut."

It wasn't *Gone With the Wind*, but as an exit line it did what it had to do. Not only had I screwed things up between Noah and me, I had also blown the case for the business. There was no mention of Malcolm, of course. Whether she knew or not, there were no questions of concern or interest and somehow what happened never came up in conversation: "Oh, Hannah, by the way, you know that guy who had a heart attack while he was boffing you? Well, he's dead."

No. Hannah was gone, without the Malcolm thing ever coming to light. Sometime during the brief dispute, Rafe must have turned around in his chair, because now he was shuffling papers on Malcolm's desk, pretending not to have noticed what had just played in front of him. My private life had been broadcast in front of my employee, and it didn't look good. According to them, I was a slut, a liar, and I'd betrayed the trust of a client. And the worst part was, it was true.

I wanted to explain to Rafe. Let him know I wasn't all that bad. Or that I'd just screwed up. Or maybe just tell someone how sorry I was. Only the words didn't come. I tried to open my mouth, but the muscles in my jaw sort of spasmed around and I wasn't making any sound and I couldn't think of anything to say and I was losing control and there were tears and I wasn't going to stop them but I was damn well not going to sob at least not till I was alone.

"How about that coffee now?"

I nodded. It was as much as I could get out without totally losing control. Rafe took off like a man reprieved from the chair, probably thanking God that I'd chosen to keep things to myself and not drag him into them any more than I had.

By the time he'd come back with coffee and a Danish, his way of letting me know he really did care, I'd pretty much pulled myself together. I still wanted to crawl home and stick my head in the oven, and I still agreed with Hannah's and Noah's general assessments of my character, but at least I could talk again and at least I'd lost the desire to bury my head in Rafe's shoulder, telling him everything I'd ever done wrong in my entire life.

Which would have left an uncomfortable silence if I hadn't decided to bring him into the case. Rafe was as glad as I was to have something besides the Lowells to talk about and listened as I ran down Wilsey's connections with dirty cops, opium, and dealing dentists. I talked about his involvement with Goenther and Evie Weber and about the book he both was and wasn't writing. How the cops would love to nail the whole thing on one of the drug situations, but what still worried me was just how my apartment and the book fit in. Rafe swallowed his coffee.

"Shoot. It's like everyone who'd kill him 'cause he wrote some sort of tell-all book didn't kill him."

It was true, and it's what I'd been thinking ever since we found Wilsey dead. Maybe it was the way he said it, though, or maybe it was just hearing it said out loud, but it suddenly occurred to me that if nobody killed Wilsey because he did write the book, someone might have killed him because he didn't.

FORTY-ONE

♦

"Hi, Nell."

She was in her father's apartment again. There'd been no trouble tracking her down at all. Only things weren't the same as the last time I'd been here. She'd buzzed me up with no difficulty. But when she opened the door, she didn't look like the same person on her way to meet her father at the club.

The hair was halfway back to the wild frizz she'd worn at

Wilsey's place. The new clothes looked dirty and worn, as if
they'd been slept in for a week. The jagged mannerisms
were on their way back.

It was like she'd been living in her father's world as long as
she could and now was beginning to return to her own. More
likely, she'd kept a few hits of speed around just in case.

"What do you want?"

There were none of the manners she'd displayed on my
last visit. No breeding. No attempt at civility.

"I'm here about Wilsey."

Nell shook out her hair, then lit up a Winston and stuck it
in a cigarette holder.

"Wilsey?"

"Your boyfriend?"

She exhaled, sending smoke dramatically in my direction.

"Oh, that. That was ages ago."

"It was last week."

She stared at me. I held my breath before speaking, wondering if it was all a shot in the dark. Wondering if I was
just frustrated that everyone else from Brotell and Sarmiento
to Frank, Rantz, Morris, and Max seemed to be clear. But
there was more. She was the one who'd first mentioned the
book, sending me looking for everyone who'd be threatened
by it. She'd been close enough to Wilsey that if the opium
dealers had offed him she certainly wouldn't have felt comfortable enough to trot upstairs to fire up like she had the
first time I'd seen her. Then there was the sudden, coinci-
dental reconciliation with her father. That and everyone else
checking out added up to something.

"You shot him, didn't you, Nell?"

There was no reaction.

"I figure you'd been counting on his writing a book."

"Why would I count on that? Are you crazy? Wilsey
could never write a book."

"Not one that could sell, maybe. But maybe he could just put down some ideas. Some names. Some places. With as much proof as possible. Just so he could scare some people."

Nell was pacing now. Listening to what I was saying, trying to focus as much as she could considering she was high.

"No. We were writing together. We were going to sell to the movies."

"You were going to sell, but not to the movies."

"I was going to be a star again."

"You were going to sell it to Wilsey's buddies on the force, wasn't that it?"

"No."

"They'd been paying him off for years. Only it wasn't that much. And Wilsey never asked for more. And all that money was just sitting there."

"No. Slow down."

"So you told him to make an informal arrangement a little more formal. You told him to blackmail the people who'd been looking after him. And just in case one of these people didn't appreciate what Wilsey was up to, you wanted Wilsey's stories to be written down. Someplace where you'd have access to them. So you could take care of yourself whatever happened to Wilsey. Without coming back to your father."

"There is nothing wrong with my father," she said. Only she was screaming when she said it.

"Only you never saw any of what he was working on, so when he said he was dropping off the book with a detective for safekeeping, you decided to follow him to my apartment. Somehow, you two came back. This time you had a gun. When you couldn't find the book, you shot him. Is that how it went, Nell?"

"Don't say anything, Nell."

Maybe it was Malcolm's death, maybe the scene I'd just had with Noah, and maybe it was just feeling like I was finally bringing the whole thing to a close, but I'd let down my guard while I was talking, and I hadn't noticed the man walk into the room.

"We'll get a lawyer. She has no proof."

He was in his early sixties, but hadn't lost his hair color. It was a tan color. Like his skin. The guy was one of those monochromatic people. One color from top to bottom. It didn't take too much guessing to figure he was the guy who owned the apartment.

Nell had seemed like she was only half-listening while I spoke, and I was afraid she'd just clam up now. She looked at her father, then took a hit from the cigarette holder. When she finally began to speak, it was barely audible.

"That son of a bitch promised me."

"Nell, stop it."

"Why?"

Her father turned to me.

"Get out. You have no right to be here. I'm calling security."

She was screaming now.

"He said he'd take care of me. That son of a bitch."

"She's a sick girl. You're taking advantage. You have no right."

"He lied to me. To me. Did he think I was stupid?"

I started to think back to the first time I met Wilsey.

"Nell, stop."

"He didn't want to rock the boat. He was weak. 'Things are fine as they are, Nell.' 'Why blow it, Nell?' "

There was no junk back then. He'd just started the whole undercover thing.

"Then he figured he'd try to quiet me down. He said he'd

write the book. He said he'd up the price. Only I never saw anything. I never saw him writing."

"Nell, you can't unsay this. There's no undoing it anymore," her father said.

"Then he came back from your place with all these ... these lies of how these cops and crims had tried to stop him, attack him. But I saw. I was watching. Oh, I let him believe I believed him. I did. Then I made him take me back. Where's the book, Wilsey? Where's the fucking book?"

I wished I'd had some better memory. Something the kid did. Something he'd said. But that's the one that came to mind. Sitting there, eating everything on his plate, no elbows on the table, calling me ma'am, the whole nine yards.

By the time Nell got to the part about blowing Wilsey's head off, Papa Weston was getting out his checkbook in an attempt to solve things the old-fashioned way. I wasn't sure what the going rate was anymore. I didn't want to know. There was no client to disappoint. If there was ever a time to bend with the wind, this was it. I let the check sit on the table. Maybe some other time.

I looked at Nell. She was still smoking with that stupid cigarette holder. That might or might not have been the whole story. Maybe there'd been a fight. Maybe the first shot had been an accident. It didn't matter. What mattered was that she'd killed Wilsey. I didn't have all that much in the way of proof. I didn't have to. I'd call Max. If he was still taking my calls. Her confession would be enough for him to bring her in. They'd take some prints, some hair and blood samples. Something would put her in my apartment, tying her into the killing. I left the building, hoping I wouldn't have to think about Wilsey or Frank or Stub Kinnon or any of it again.

FORTY-TWO

◆

It was a simple junkie murder. About nothing more than junkie dreams. Only the junkie who'd been killed happened to be an ex-cop who'd gotten dirty. His death and the investigation that resulted scared at least a couple of cops and a dentist and inspired one low-life junkie burglar to take his shot at the brass ring. Only Bobby Sarmiento would never have figured cops to have enough money to make Wilsey take the blackmail gamble. He must have figured Wilsey'd be more into drugs, Pushing whatever information he had into a piece of the action. Maybe a nice little dealership in the right kind of neighborhood. Maybe even a position in the opium operation. Sarmiento'd probably angled for the same kind of deal for himself. Only he'd figured wrong and that had gotten him killed. It was that kind of case. It had even forced me to get back in touch with an ex-husband who was falling apart and gave him the opportunity to fall apart on me.

Enough. It was seven o'clock. Just enough time to make it to the hospital before it closed. I hadn't spoken to anyone about whatever arrangements would have to be made. I wasn't sure if I would be the one to make them. Maybe some relative would crawl out of the woodwork and handle the whole thing. Maybe once they'd shown up, they'd never want to leave.

It was hard to believe Malcolm was gone. Ever since Rafe

had told me, I'd been acting like he was just sick. The business was in my hands, sure. But I was only handling it until he came back. I kept thinking he was up and about and hassling nurses. Sending out for food the doctor told him to avoid. Calling Hannah Lowell up for one more go-around.

I hadn't dealt with the death of anyone close for some time. How long would it take before I stopped being surprised the door was still locked when I got there in the morning? How many times would I buy an extra cup of coffee on my way up? Who would I turn to to talk things over with? Hell, I'd probably even miss worrying about how to fend off the guy's advances without getting into some sort of fight.

It would have been great to have gone out on a better note. It would be even better to have someone to go get drunk with and talk about Malcolm and old times. There was Rafe, of course, but he hated the old guy and they didn't really have much in the way of old times. There were some of Malcolm's old cronies, too. But they'd probably want to sit around and crack dirty jokes. I'd only ruin their good time. My good-byes would have to be private.

That would leave me with Noah. He probably wouldn't take my call. That was okay. I knew where he lived. And if he wasn't home, I'd sit there until he was. I was a detective. I could stake him out. There wasn't much else to say, of course. "Sorry" would pretty much wrap it up. There'd be an explanation. There'd be tears. I'd see where things went from there. It was my experience that begging forgiveness never accomplished much. If Noah was inclined to give it another try, he'd do it without the begging. If he wasn't, the begging wouldn't help. I hoped he was.

That was as far ahead as I could think right now. Only

when I got to the hospital, I wasn't quite ready to face up to things. I could have grabbed some dried-out club sandwich at the coffee shop or browsed through the books at the gift shop that hadn't been current when they first arrived, but when I saw a bank of phones in the hallway, I got the sudden urge to call Evie Weber. She'd be glad to know those phone calls would be stopping. Death threats had a way of taking the fun out of life. And, what the hell, while I had her on the phone, maybe I'd see if she wanted to meet me for lunch. I hadn't had someone to talk with for some time now. It certainly couldn't do me any harm.